ESCAPE FROM
ALCATRAZ

ANDY MARINO

Scholastic Inc.

Library of Congress Cataloging-in-Publication Data
Names: Marino, Andy, 1980– author.
Title: Escape from Alcatraz / Andy Marino.
Description: New York : Scholastic Inc., 2024. | Series: Escape from ; 4 | Summary: In 1962 Chip Carter, son of a guard at Alcatraz, stumbles on to an escape plan and finds himself forced to aid the prisoners, because he is afraid that his father is somehow involved in the plot—and he needs to find out the truth.
Identifiers: LCCN 2024003491 (print) | LCCN 2024003492 (ebook) | ISBN 9781338858587 (paperback) | ISBN 9781338858594 (ebook)
Subjects: LCSH: United States Penitentiary, Alcatraz Island, California—Juvenile fiction. | Prisons—California—Alcatraz Island—Officials and employees—Juvenile fiction. | Escapes—California –Alcatraz Island—Juvenile fiction. | Fathers and sons—Juvenile fiction. | Alcatraz Island (Calif.)—Juvenile fiction. | CYAC: Prisons—Fiction. | Escapes—Fiction. | Fathers and sons—Fiction. | Alcatraz Island (Calif.)—Fiction. | California—History—20th century—Fiction. | Mystery and detective stories. | BISAC: JUVENILE FICTION / Historical / United States / 20th Century | JUVENILE FICTION / Mysteries & Detective Stories | LCGFT: Historical fiction. | Detective and mystery fiction. | Novels.
Classification: LCC PZ7.M33877 Es 2024 (print) | LCC PZ7.M33877 (ebook) | DDC 813.6 [Fic]—dc23/eng/20240125

10 9 8 7 6 5 4 3 2 1   24 25 26 27 28

Printed in the U.S.A.   40
First printing 2024

Book design by Christopher Stengel

FOR LEVI & ASA

CHAPTER

The bay is angry.

As a boat, the *Warden Johnston*, slides along a swell, the bow pitches up, and spray lashes the windows of the cabin. The choppy surface heaves and rolls beneath Chip Carter's feet. He glances up the aisle at his fellow passengers. Nobody looks scared. Every school day, they make the trip to San Francisco and back.

The boat is the only way off Alcatraz Island. Even if the crossing is rough, they are lucky they get to make it at all. Most residents of the Rock can never leave.

Chip moves a toothpick from one side of his mouth to the other. It tastes a bit like pine. Like he's snacking on a tree.

"Go on," he says to the girl perched on the edge of the wooden bench across the aisle. Matilda Thompson, who everyone calls Maddie. A fellow sixth grader on her way back from school in the city across the bay. Her brown hair is tightly trapped by a green headband that makes Chip think of parrot feathers.

Maddie glances up the aisle. She leans forward so far she's almost bent in half at the waist, hands clasped on her knees. She works nervously at a silver ring on her pinkie, twisting and taking it off and slipping it back on. Thunder rolls across the water. The smell of the sea—brine and salt and endless depths—invades the cabin.

"It's about Albert," she whispers.

Chip takes in the name, rolls it around in his mind. It lands with an unpleasant thud. Albert McCain, a seventh grader with a voice as deep as his dad's.

Albert's seated in the front of the cabin, stretching out a wad of chewing gum, trying to stick it to the window. Just above him, a poster on the door to the pilothouse says FIRE IS SABOTAGE!

"I knew this case was gonna be a doozy," Chip says. "Knew it from the minute you walked into my office."

Maddie frowns, puzzled, and looks around. Chip waits patiently. One day he'll be a real detective with a real office. For now, the back of the boat will have to do.

"Anyway," Maddie says, "the thing is, Albert's been pretty mean to my brother since last summer."

"Shakedowns," Chip says.

"What?"

"Lunch money."

"Oh. Yes. He's been taking the dimes our mother gives us for lunch."

"Small change."

"I guess."

"But it adds up." Chip takes out a small notebook and flips to a blank page. "Fifty cents a week."

"It's hard to understand you with that toothpick in your mouth, Chip."

"It helps me think. Listen, Maddie, I can't fight Albert McCain. If your brother doesn't want to tell on Albert—"

"He's not a snitch!"

"—then I don't know what I can do for you."

Chip thinks of himself as a pretty normal-size sixth grader. Albert is nearly a foot taller, with broad shoulders and hands that swallow up a football at recess. The wispy beginnings of a mustache ghost his upper lip. Chip watches Albert give up on the window experiment and stick the gum behind his ear for later. The backs of his classmates' heads move with the rolling of the boat. Chip's gaze bounces along polka-dotted kerchiefs, baseball caps, slicked hair parted ruler-straight. Fifty kids, the children of officers and prison guards, growing up on a cold, rocky island. Outside, the storm swirls into a roiling mass of gray. It's like the ship has sailed into a cloud.

"It's the not the lunch money I'm here about," Maddie says.

"All right," Chip says. He waits quietly for Maddie to continue. Except for the way he works the toothpick around in his mouth, he sits perfectly still. Like all his methods, he learned this one from the private investigator Jake Hall, hero of the ABC crime drama *Hall of Justice*. It's now halfway through season two of the show, and Chip has seen every one of its fifty-seven episodes. Jake Hall knows that when a new client walks into his office, it's best to let the person air their thoughts without too much prodding. That way you learn things they might not have intended to give away. You build the truth of the matter with little scraps of information.

"It's the raincoats," Maddie says.

"The raincoats." Chip tamps down his excitement. He can already tell this is shaping up to be a real case. He plays it cool, meets Maddie's eyes.

"Yeah," she says. "My brother and I got these sharp new slickers last Christmas. Yellow and blue. You can turn them inside out and still wear them. The material's nice and thick. Sturdy. Almost like boots."

"I know the ones you mean," Chip says. He's seen Benny and Maddie Thompson waiting on the gangplank to board the ship, wearing their matching slickers. "Real nice."

She nods. "Not flimsy like some of them."

"All show and no go."

"Well, now they're gone."

"Gone how?"

"Stolen."

"At school?"

"At home. One day they were hanging in the closet, the next day they weren't."

Chip mulls this over. It wouldn't be hard to steal from a family that lives on Alcatraz. Nobody locks their doors. Most of the doors don't even *have* locks. It's like Chip's father says: *There's no crime in our neighborhood. We already know where all the criminals are.*

Living on an island that's home to America's most notorious prison—and its most fearsome prisoners—is a good reminder to keep on the straight and narrow. You want to stay on the side of the law that's allowed to take a boat across the bay. To one day have a future off the island.

But that doesn't mean some kids don't take risks.

"You suspect Albert," Chip says.

"Who else?"

Jake Hall wouldn't get ahead of things with guesswork. He'd wait for the facts to steer his investigation. "Could be anyone who lives on the island with us," Chip points out.

"Well, it wasn't me."

"Right now, everyone's a suspect."

Maddie pauses. A wave splashes up the side of the boat. Water slides in crooked fingers down the windows. "I didn't take my own raincoat, Chip. That wouldn't even be stealing." She sits up straight. "Dara Pearce told me you were a real detective. She said you found her kitten."

"Mr. Mustache," Chip says. "My first case."

Cats and dogs are technically not allowed on the island, but Dara had snuck back a stray from the city, inside her coat. When it wandered off a few days later, Chip had tracked the kitten to one of the neighborhood gardens. He'd discovered her trembling beneath some rhododendrons and given her back to Dara without alerting any of the adults. In the way of island rumor mills, word had spread among his classmates that Chip Carter was a bona fide private eye.

So Chip had stepped into the role of a lifetime.

Maddie folds her arms and turns to look out the window. Chip follows her gaze as Alcatraz Island slides into view. Green-and-black rocks rise from the bay like the hump of some giant undersea creature frozen in place. The tall white spire of the lighthouse juts up through the misty rain. The large block of the penitentiary's main cell house, with its long rows of narrow windows, looks almost pink beneath the heavy clouds.

Pummeled by the storm, the island appears even more forbidding than usual. On days like today, Chip can scarcely believe anyone lives out here, in the middle of a bay racked by harsh wind and thick fog. But live out here they do—Chip and the other kids whose fathers guard the "incorrigibles" of the United States prison system. The gangsters and killers and escape artists that other prisons on the mainland simply could not contain. The worst of the worst.

Chip has lived in one of the cottages on the southern tip of the island ever since he was very little. And with his father's new promotion to senior guard, he won't be leaving anytime soon—not until he's old enough to make up his own mind about where he lives and what he does.

He imagines one day having his own place in the city. One of the new high-rises going up downtown. His name on a frosted glass door like Jake Hall's.

CHIP CARTER—PRIVATE DETECTIVE

Five and a half more years until he turns eighteen. An eternity on this island.

"Hey, Maddie."

She turns to look at him. He plucks the toothpick from his mouth and snaps it in half.

"I'll take the case."

CHAPTER

The storm dies at dusk. Chip looks out across the water at the hazy Bay Bridge, rust colored in the fading light. The bridge sprouts northeast from the edge of San Francisco and connects the city to Oakland, too far away for Chip to see from his house. The setting sun sends flecks of gold dancing across the bay. A cargo ship in the distance blows its horn on its way into port.

Chip drinks his chocolate milk in silence. His father will be at work, in the prison up on the hill, until well past dinnertime. Chip wipes milk away from his upper lip with the back of his hand. Outside, a seabird lands in one of the big messy trees at the edge of the cottage's small backyard, where the rocks slant down sharply to the water. The bird preens itself with quick, darting movements, then lifts off. Chip watches until it is nothing but a dim V shape pasted to the darkening sky.

Next door, the four Harrison kids are making a racket. Chip catches a blur of motion in the backyard as the twins, Patsy and Lenny, play one of their strange made-up sports. A football and a basketball collide in midair.

The neighboring cottages are all like this, bursting with the energy of the large families within. There are several of these houses reserved for veteran guards huddled together at the island's southern tip. But only this cottage, inhabited solely by Chip and his father, is mostly quiet. Except for the television at night.

In a little while, Patsy and Lenny will be called in for dinner. Then Chip will go to the fridge and pull out the tray his father prepared before he left for work. There will be instructions on a note: the oven temperature and time it will take for Chip to reheat the meal.

For a man who never cooked much before his wife—Chip's mother—passed away, Hiram Carter is a pretty good chef. Even if he can only make five things. Today is Friday, so Chip knows it will be swordfish and green beans.

He drains his glass and lets impressions of the past day wash over him. The fog-shrouded city, the hum of the boat's engine as they headed out for school. The walk from the pier down the Embarcadero, where Alcatraz kids join city kids for classes.

Today in math, he'd been called to the board to solve an equation. After he scrawled the answer and dropped the chalk in its tray, a strange thing happened. As he turned away from the board, time seemed to slow down. Twenty-seven of his fellow students locked eyes on him. The expressions on their faces were troubling. Not because anyone was giving him the stink eye, or sneering, or sticking out their tongue. But because they were unreadable, even to a detective. Chip ought to be able to read faces like the ingredients on the side of a cereal box. Interpret curled lips and narrowed eyes like an expert translator. Yet he can never tell what other kids think of him. Nobody seems to dislike him outright, but neither does anyone go out of their way to include him in games at recess or on the parade grounds.

He gets the feeling that for his classmates, he is just sort of *there*. And he can't figure out what he has done, or not done, to earn this status.

He tells himself that his classmates respect him for finding Dara's cat and keeping it a secret. But respect is what friends give each other—right? So why doesn't he have anybody he can really call a friend?

He breathes in and out, in and out. Friday afternoons are odd and restless. There's no reason to crack the books for homework—that's what Sunday nights are for. Later, he'll meet his father at the social hall, where most of the island gathers on Fridays. But for the next few hours, Chip has no place to be and no one to answer to. He tells himself that he likes it this way. Jake Hall is a man of solitude, habit, and routine. It's how a private eye does his work: alone, haunting the shadows, lost in thought.

Chip tells himself that it's a superpower, knowing how to be alone. There is something about it that makes him feel ready to grow up.

He goes into the kitchen and rinses his glass. Then he sits down at the table. In the center is a bowl of apples and pears. Next to the bowl is his notebook. He flips it open to the page he began earlier today.

The case of the stolen raincoats.

He taps his pencil on the table. Then he starts a sketch from memory. Maddie's rain slicker, identical to her brother's, which has also apparently been stolen.

Or misplaced, he reminds himself.

Or simply lost.

He might be working with a new client, but that doesn't mean he can automatically trust her.

After all, what if she hired him for nefarious purposes? It happens all the time on *Hall of Justice*. Scam artists and flimflam men and shady heiresses who try to rope Jake Hall into their little games.

A sudden knock at the front door startles him. Nobody ever comes over when his dad's not here. In the first weeks after his mom died, the other guards' wives would stop by with casseroles and pies, but those visits have long since stopped.

He gets up from the table and heads down the hall, past the framed portrait of his mother and the antique cuckoo clock. Yesterday's *San Francisco Chronicle* is tossed on the table next to the front door, alongside a little glass bowl of stray pennies and a black button from his father's guard uniform. President Kennedy smiles boyishly out from a photograph on the front page of the *Chronicle*. The caption says he's in a place called Hyannis Port.

KNOCK-KNOCK-KNOCK.

Louder now. Insistent.

Chip pauses. Something doesn't feel right. Pressure between his eyes moves down the tip of his nose. A tingling sort of warning. In the city, doors are often equipped with little peepholes so you can see who's standing outside. Not here, though.

Suddenly, the unlocked door flies open.

A tall, skinny kid takes one step inside the house. Benny Thompson. His unruly mop is the same dark shade as his younger sister Maddie's. His face is pinched in anxious determination.

The tickle in Chip's nose subsides. There's nothing dangerous about Benny Thompson. The seventh grader is known for being constantly in motion—feet tapping, legs bouncing, body twisting this way and that at his school desk. Even now, standing in Chip's front hall, there's something jumpy and nervous about him. He throws a quick glance over his shoulder as if someone's lurking at his back.

Chip peers outside the open door behind the boy. The path from the parade ground to the cottage is swallowed up by deepening shadows.

"Benny," Chip says. He tries to be cordial. "Hey."

There's a pause. Benny meets his eyes for a moment, then looks at the cuckoo clock.

"Do you want some chocolate milk?" Chip asks.

"I don't have time," Benny says. He scratches the side of his head. Then he tries to smile, but it comes out crinkly and forced. "Um," he says.

"Are you okay?"

Benny shuts the door behind him, slowly and carefully, as if he's trying not to wake someone in the house. He turns to Chip, clasps his hands together in front of him, then unclasps them and holds his arms straight down at his sides.

"I know my sister talked to you today," he says.

Chip frowns. Now that he's been hired by Maddie, he's obligated to keep her confidence. He can't disclose any information, even to her own brother.

Or her parents.

Chip doesn't nod or shrug. He doesn't move a muscle. He just waits for Benny to say what he came to say.

He thinks of the notebook, left open on the kitchen table.

Chip's silence seems to drive Benny up the wall. His cheek throbs. His lip twitches. His hands curl into fists. Finally, he blurts it out.

"Just forget what she said, okay?"

Chip thinks about this for a moment. "Is there something you want to tell me, Benny?"

Benny's eyes widen. "I just told you! Maddie doesn't know what she's talking about."

"I'll keep that in mind. You going bowling later?"

Benny sputters. Then his face goes slack. His shoulders sag. For once, he is completely still. Chip is taken aback by how sad he looks.

"Please, Chip," he says. "Just stay out of it."

It, thinks Chip. Meaning, *something*. Meaning, *this case has juice*.

He thinks of Albert taking Benny's lunch money. Hassling him every day on the walk from the pier to the school. *This kid is scared.*

Chip doesn't blame him. He would be scared, too, if he became Albert's prime target.

"All right," Chip agrees.

Benny looks suspicious. He narrows his eyes.

"All *right*," Chip says again.

Benny perks up. The hint of a smile comes across his face. "Okay," he says once, to himself. Then, to Chip: "Okay, thanks!" He practically spins on his heel and leaps to open the door. "See you later!" he calls out before heading down the path.

Chip goes back into the kitchen. An elevator-drop feeling gathers in his belly. The tingle in his nose spreads down his neck to warm his chest.

He sits down at the table and records the incident in his notebook.

5:27 p.m. Visit from Benny Thompson. Tried to warn me off the case.

He tells himself he feels bad for lying to Benny. But Jake Hall would not drop a case for any reason, and he's been chased down alleys, beaten up, and even shot at by folks who would rather not be investigated.

Whenever someone pressures Jake Hall to drop a case, it means there's more to it than meets the eye.

Chip's excitement jumbles his thoughts. He drinks a glass of water, then opens the fridge and takes out a plate wrapped in tinfoil. Taped to the foil is his dad's usual note:

Dear Chipper,

Preheat oven to 350. Heat up food for 20 minutes. WEAR A MITT AND TURN OVEN OFF AFTERWARD.

I will see you later tonight at the social hall.

I was thinking today that we ought to go to more baseball games this year. What do you think about that?

Love you, pal.

—Dad

PS You can invite a friend!

CHAPTER

3

The social hall on Alcatraz is a short walk north from the cottages. Chip takes his time in the cool night air, moving along the pathway that snakes around the middle of the island. Below him is the pier where the *Warden Johnston* is docked. Above him, on the big rock, the prison rises in all its drab glory.

He strolls past Building 64, the three-story apartment block that houses most of the guards and their families. Maddie and Benny Thompson live there with their parents. Albert McCain does, too. Chip knows he's lucky to inhabit one of the cottages. Yet as he passes Building 64, he stops to take in the lighted windows and something within him stirs. Figures move past in shadow. Televisions glow with shifting shapes. Chip transports himself inside, his senses moving like a soft breeze through the corridors. Cooking smells and dish soap and the bickering of brothers and sisters. Doorways connecting friends and neighbors. Card games and borrowed toys and books passed down the hall.

It might be nice to live in a lively place like Building 64.

He breathes deep. Sea air, of course, but other things, too. Scents swept across the bay from the city—freshly cut grass and fried food.

Laughter from a passing tourist boat.

Chip looks up the dark face of the rock that rises on his left. Atop this massive plateau sits the main cell house. He wonders if the inmates can hear what he can hear, smell what he smells. Little hints of freedom, drifting into the cellblocks. The very idea gives him a bleak and empty feeling. Loneliness more gnawing and terrible than any long and solitary afternoon.

The wind kicks up. He thrusts his hands into the pockets of his tan jacket. Three boys and two girls burst out the front door of the apartment building. High school kids. He catches a whiff of perfume. They ignore him as they head up the path toward the social hall. He clutches his notebook in his pocket. One of the older girls turns and walks backward, slowly, as she calls out to him.

"Hi there, Chip!"

He waves. "Hi, Susie." He doesn't know Susie Porter at all, except by name.

"You coming to the hall?"

"In a minute."

"You want to walk with us?"

One of the boys reaches for the sleeve of her coat. "What's the difference? Not like he's gonna get lost." He gives Chip a glance. "Ain't that right?"

"That's right," Chip says.

"See? He's fine." The boy pulls her sleeve and she turns her back on Chip. Holding hands, they hurry into the night to catch their friends.

Chip follows slowly, his feet crunching gravel and bits of rock scattered along the path. He wonders what would have happened if he'd said *sure* and joined the older kids. At least it would have given him an opportunity to observe how they act around one another.

Chip knows it's strange, to study friendship like it's an ant farm in science class. He's pretty sure those high school kids don't spend time analyzing *how* to be friends. They just *are* friends.

He flashes to earlier, at school, when he'd turned to find the whole class looking at him with unreadable expressions. It's like a dream now.

A few minutes later the lights of the social hall come into view. The white building looks like an old Spanish mission, with its sloped roof and wide-open balcony. Supported by white pillars, the upper floor cascades over the side of the rock face. The lower floor opens out onto the path by the water below. Music comes from inside: Elvis Presley's "Good Luck Charm."

That means the high school kids are in charge of the radio

tonight. The adults favor softer crooning with orchestra sections.

It isn't until Chip is nearly at the door that the big kid steps out of the shadows to block his way.

Albert McCain.

Chip glances to either side. There's no one else out here.

"Hey, Carter," Albert says. There's a softness to his voice— almost a gentleness—that Chip finds alarming. The boy is lit from above by a lamp that hangs above the entrance. His round face swims in deep shadows. The tips of his buzz cut sparkle, coarse hairs catching the light.

"Hi, Albert," Chip says. Rumors and gossip travel at light speed on the island. Every kid on the boat probably knows about Maddie's visit to his office in the back seat.

He really needs a more private office.

Five and a half more years.

Chip's fists clench inside his pockets. He's watched boxing matches on television: Cassius Clay, Sonny Liston, Floyd Patterson. He's practiced shadowboxing around the empty cottage and even in the mirror, his scrawny arms extending and withdrawing, all sharp elbows and skinny wrists. He's even tried pummeling his father's heavy punching bag. He can barely make it swing. Punching another person? Forget about it. Anyway, with a kid as big as Albert McCain, it would be like a mosquito slapping a bear.

Oh well. Jake Hall gets beat up in practically every episode. Chip tells himself it won't be the end of the world.

Albert doesn't move. His big frame fills the doorway. Inside, the song ends and a new one begins: "Dream Baby" by Roy Orbison.

"So how's sixth grade going?" Albert says.

"Slowly."

Albert snorts. "Mr. Franconi's a snooze." He imitates a low, droning voice. *"Turn to page forty-six in your textbooks."*

Chip likes Mr. Franconi, but he nods his head warily. "Good impression." He moves very slightly to one side to see if anyone is hanging out beyond the doorway. Someone he can pretend to be meeting up with.

"Roger's sick," Albert says, folding his arms. Chip thinks for a moment. Albert's talking about Roger Pettys, another seventh grader. "I need a partner for bowling."

"I'm more of a pool player myself," Chip says.

"I've seen you on the lanes."

"I'm not very good. It won't be much of a game."

Albert grins and his crooked teeth give him a jack-o'-lantern smile. "Not somebody to go against. A *partner*, I said. Me and Roger were supposed to bowl against the Harrisons."

Chip thinks of the two little scamps racing in madcap patterns around the backyard next door, scattering toys. "Patsy and Lenny?"

Albert snorts again. "The older ones, dingbat. Kenneth and Mary."

"That makes more sense."

Albert's arm darts out. His hand is like an iron claw holding Chip's shoulder. His eyes are two bright tiny pebbles. His teeth flash. "Whaddaya say, Carter?" The iron claw tightens. "You and me." The voice is still soft. Chip could almost mistake it for friendly if he didn't know better. "It'll give us a chance to catch up. You can tell me all about the detective business."

At the word *detective*, something clicks in Chip's brain.

He realizes that he's not being a very good private eye right now. Shirking his duty to his client. The mystery is just starting to cook following Benny's unexpected visit to his house, and now he's bumped into an actual person of interest in the case.

Chip knows one thing: Jake Hall wouldn't be wasting this opportunity.

He pulls a toothpick from his pocket. "That's good. Because I'm working a new case, and I need to ask you a few questions." He fixes the toothpick between his teeth.

"Sure you do." Albert's eyes flash. "I'm the usual suspect around here."

"I can't rule anybody out," Chip says. "Not yet."

Albert leans in close and lowers his voice. "You think you're real swell, don't you, Carter?" Quicker than Chip thought possible, Albert snatches the toothpick from Chip's mouth and tosses it to the ground. "Playing detective." He pokes a thick finger into Chip's chest. "Sticking your nose where it don't belong. You think I don't know what Maddie said to you on the boat today? You think there are any secrets on this island?"

Chip's heart pounds. He doesn't know if Albert's getting worked up because he's hiding something, or because he's genuinely mad about being a suspect. Chip decides it's worth taking a punch to wind him up a little more and see how it all shakes out.

"Don't go ape, McCain. I'm just doing my job."

Albert opens his mouth. His grip tightens on Chip's shoulder. Chip braces himself. Then Albert lets him go. "You really are a piece of work, Carter." He pauses. "Listen good: I didn't take any stupid raincoats. And I don't know who did."

Chip brushes off the front of his shirt even though it's not dirty.

Albert stares him down. "Bowl with me or stay out here by yourself. I don't care." With that, Albert turns and heads inside. Chip watches him go. He wonders if he played that all wrong.

A sudden shout comes down from the prison. If Chip listens hard, he can hear an inmate strumming a guitar, another singing in a deep warbly voice that clashes with the music inside the social hall. Rooted to the ground, he lets it all wash over him. He can't bring himself to follow Albert inside, nor can he bring himself to go home. In this moment he feels like a true child of Alcatraz: free as the seabirds that roost on the rocks, trapped as the men in their cells on the hill.

CHAPTER

INSIDE

The lights come up on Broadway, the main corridor between B and C blocks. The morning bell rings. The hands of the round clock on the wall below the west gun gallery indicate six thirty. The sounds of a prison coming to life percolate up and down the halls. Bare feet hit the clammy floor. Toilets flush.

In cell 138 on B block, the Watcher opens his eyes. He has not been asleep. His nights are full of feverish activity. Sometimes it feels like he dreams it all. Then in the morning he checks his work when he is sure he is alone. And every time he smiles inwardly with the quiet satisfaction that has buoyed him through twenty years of confinement—National Training School for Boys in Washington, Louisiana State Penitentiary, USP Atlanta, and now Alcatraz.

Alcatraz is the only one he has not tried to escape from.

Not yet, anyway.

The Watcher eyes his accordion case shoved against the wall. He lets that inward smile take shape, thinking of the nocturnal labors the case hides. With the practiced, routine motions of the longtime prisoner, the Watcher sweeps the floor of his cell—nine feet long and five feet wide—splashes his face with water from the basin, and gets dressed. He tucks in his shirt with care. A moment later the second morning bell rings. The Watcher stands by his cell door facing the long corridor. The guards move past, counting inmates.

When the lieutenant confirms the count and gives the whistle signal, the cell doors slide open on their tracks. At the second whistle, the Watcher steps out of his cell and turns to face the dining hall. He is relaxed and calm. Facts and figures go dancing past his waking mind. Cellblock B is 150 feet long. There are three tiers. Twenty-eight cells per tier. He waits with the other inmates in a row. At the third whistle the line moves toward the dining hall.

For the next few minutes, lines form, break apart, and re-form according to the serving rules. The Watcher moves smoothly through the routine, barely conscious of how he is being shuffled this way and that by instinct alone. He serves himself eggs and sausage and toast from the steam tables. The food here is better than in USP Atlanta. They say it is the best in the whole United States prison system, and he is not inclined to argue, based on his experience. The Watcher sits down at a square cafeteria-style table. These new tables replaced the old bench tables just last year. He is joined by three other men. All of them sit with their backs perfectly straight. At the next whistle they begin eating.

They will have twenty minutes. Conversation rises all around them. Scraps and snatches of words between rapid-fire eating. Forks and spoons scrape and clank against trays. The Watcher takes the measure of his three companions.

John and Clarence Anglin. A pair of bank-robbing brothers he knows from his time at USP Atlanta. An inseparable pair of look-alikes, except John is fair-haired to Clarence's brown. Both keep neat sideburns. If you met them on the outside, you would peg them for insurance salesmen or the employees of an advertising agency. Unless, of course, you were a bank teller and they were sticking a gun in your face and demanding cash. The warden even allows them adjacent cells down the row from the Watcher on the ground-floor tier, 150 and 152. The Watcher trusts them as much as he trusts anybody, which is not very much.

The fourth man at the table is Allen West. The Watcher's next-door neighbor in cell 140. A thin man with penetrating eyes and the permanent hint of a smirk, he is in Alcatraz for stealing cars and driving them across state lines. The Watcher is not sure what to make of West—he is smart, which is good, but he is also the kind of person who wants everyone to know that he is smart, which is bad. Either way, the Watcher and the Anglin brothers are stuck with him: It was West who set everything in motion when he discovered an old ventilator hole in the ceiling of C block that had not been properly cemented shut.

The Watcher swallows a bite of scrambled eggs. "I got word from Red," he says—their nickname for one of the guards who serve as their link to the outside. He keeps his voice low and chews at odd intervals between sentences. Anybody looking at their table would notice idle conversation. Nothing important. The other men barely look up from their food as they listen to his report. John Anglin dabs egg bits from the corner of his mouth with a napkin.

"The test raft is seaworthy all right," he says. "It'll work. He used some type of resin to join the raincoats."

"Resin?" Clarence Anglin says. "We can't get resin in here."

"Shops have liquid plastic," West offers.

"Close enough," the Watcher says. "Red's trying out a new method to inflate it, too. He'll test it this weekend."

John Anglin sips coffee. Clarence bites down on a sausage link. West, a speedy eater, scrapes his plate—the kind of man one of his many foster mothers would have remarked had a "hollow leg." The Watcher regards the men at the table. Thrown together by Alcatraz—a small island prison that sponges up the would-be escape artists the other prisons cannot hold.

People on the outside think of prison life as drab and unchanging, and in many ways it is. But when you are a person like the Watcher with a restless roving mind, for whom all the crosswords and brainteasers and puzzles can barely whet the appetite, there is always one looming proposition that pulls you forward through the days.

Escape.

The Watcher does not think he is special. He is a common criminal from a broken home. No different from most of the men he has met on the inside. But sometimes, at night, when he is digging away at the cement that surrounds the vent at the back of his cell, he thinks there must be some kind of invisible force—call it destiny, call it luck—that has lined things up to help him succeed.

Take the Anglin brothers: Here, they find themselves together again, after meeting in Atlanta. What are the odds? And his next-door neighbor, West—the man is teaching him accordion, which gave the Watcher the idea to use the instrument case to hide his work on the vent.

So he is not special. Or blessed. But he is smart enough to seize an opportunity when he is presented with one.

Carefully, quietly, the four men finish breakfast and discuss the other details of their plan. The Watcher can sense West's leg going up and down a mile a minute underneath the table. He reads twitches of excitement on Clarence Anglin's face. His own heartbeat is steady. He looks to an observer like a man resigned to doing his time. He wishes he could impose some of his patience on his collaborators. After all, there is still so much work to do. It is not like they will be busting out tonight. Every step must be carefully plotted, all the angles considered. His ideal partners in this operation would be three other versions of himself. But he has to make do with what has been given to him.

The Watcher places his knife on the left side of his tray, his fork in the middle, his spoon on the right. He sits straight-backed as the guards walk past, checking that no utensils are missing. The men rise at the whistle to begin their day. Same as yesterday and the day before that and the day before that . . .

CHAPTER

5

Saturday afternoon passes in a blur of bad weather and worse television. Chip sits through old reruns of *The Adventures of Rin Tin Tin* and *The Roy Rogers Show*. There's a new *Watch Mr. Wizard* on at noon, but the subject is rocks. He switches to the news.

The Soviets launched a satellite. The US Navy declared an airplane missing over the Pacific.

He scribbles idly in his notebook, turning over the elements of the case.

Benny, acting scared, warning him to drop it.

Albert, acting like Albert, telling Chip he had nothing to do with it.

Chip is troubled by how everyone on Alcatraz Island knows

his business. He feels like he's living in a fishbowl. Like the walls of the cottage are see-through, and all his classmates are lurking outside in the storm, peering in. He sips his chocolate milk and thinks.

When Jake Hall feels the weight of the city pressing down on him, depicted in the opening credits of *Hall of Justice* as skyscrapers with leering faces, he finds a way to change the game. It's like putting all the pieces of a case into a plastic cup, shaking them like dice, and seeing what you roll. Leaving it up to fate as a way to advance the investigation. A little bit of chance, a little bit of luck.

Problem is, Chip's never been the lucky type.

A rhythmic series of thwacks comes from upstairs. His father is hitting the heavy bag. With so much extra space in the cottage, he's turned the spare room into an exercise studio. There's a rack of metal dumbbells, a bench, and boxing equipment. Many of the guards are out of shape, huffing and puffing all over the island, but not Hiram Carter. *THWACK.* Chip's father is still built like the boxer he'd been after he got out of the army. *THWACK.* Chip has seen the photographs. *THWACK.* His father always had tons of friends. *THWACK.* His photo albums from every stage of his life prove it.

Teenagers hanging out on the backs of cars with big fins.

Army buddies with rolled-up sleeves and lopsided smiles.

Work pals at barbecues on the deck of the social hall.

Chip flips his notebook closed and looks around the living room. The dusty bookshelf full of the thick novels his mother liked to read. The carved wooden birds in motionless flight along the wall. His father's weird little succulent plant. He drains his glass and turns his attention to the TV.

The story on the news is about an FBI wiretap that led to some gangsters being arrested in Chicago. One of the agents is being interviewed with his face hidden in shadow.

"When we needed to rattle their cages a little bit," the agent says, "we'd tickle the wire."

He goes on to explain that *tickling the wire* means slipping one of the gangsters some juicy gossip, then listening in as he fed it to his associates on the wiretap.

Chip gets up from the shag carpet in front of the TV. That's it: the tactic he needs. He's not going to get anywhere hiding from the rain, scribbling in his notebook. He's gotta pound the pavement. Rattle some cages.

Tickle the wire.

"I'm going for a walk!" he calls upstairs. The thwacks subside.

"It's raining!" his father calls down. Chip can hear him breathing hard. His workouts have gotten more intense over the past few months. Like he's trying to bash his way to some new place.

"It's always raining!"

There's a pause as his father considers this, then a thwack as he resumes striking the heavy bag.

Chip's father is always more talkative in the notes he leaves for Chip than in real life.

Chip opens the front hall closet, wood paneled to blend into the wall beneath the staircase. President Kennedy's brother

Robert smiles up from the newspaper folded on the table next to the dish of pennies. Chip peers into the closet. He's struck by the scent of his mother's old coat—one of her many possessions his father never got around to packing away. It smells like the sea, like the spray that cascades up the side of the boat. Chip remembers weekend trips to the city with her—always the best in winter, when the shop windows shone with strands of lights glinting off piles of fake snow. He reaches out and lays a hand on the thick wool fabric. Then he shakes off the memory and grabs his rain slicker.

Outside the cottage, the parade ground is empty. The cement expanse that covers the southern tip of the island serves as the kids' football field, baseball diamond, racecourse, and all-purpose hangout zone. The rain is a light mist while the fog hangs in thick sheets. Chip can barely see the stately residence of the associate warden. The apartments across the parade ground—buildings A, B, and C—are completely obscured by the gray soup.

The gut-rumbling blast of the foghorn drifts mournfully across the grounds. Chip shoves his hands in his pockets and takes a right up the path, retracing his steps from last night. He decides, all at once, that he's going to knock on the Thompsons' door. He's going to tell Benny that the raincoat thief has been identified. That it's just a matter of time before the culprit is exposed. Then he's going to keep a close eye on Benny. See who the spooked boy runs to first. Follow the lead up the chain.

Tickle the wire.

At the southern end of the apartment building, a cement

staircase leads down to a damp and dismal alley. Legend has it that it led to a dungeon back in the island's old military prison days, a hundred years ago.

It's here that movement catches his eye: a quick flash of yellow and blue.

The colors of the missing raincoats.

A figure moves quickly down the steps and out of sight. The raincoats trail from the man's side, as if he's holding them in his fist and letting the sleeves dangle.

Instantly, the doldrums of a lonely Saturday vanish. Chip is on the hunt. Forget about tickling the wire to generate a lead—this is a genuine break in the case.

He moves quickly and quietly to the top of the staircase. The figure vanishes into the darkness below. Even when the sun's out, the dungeon alley is dim. Today it's like descending into a world of night. He pads down the stairs on tiptoes. A chill wraps around him, the damp slithering up his sleeves and curling around his neck.

Chip is suddenly aware of how defenseless he really is.

Jake Hall carries a small wooden club wrapped in leather.

In his pockets, Chip's hands make fists he doesn't know how to use. He forces himself to be silent. Takes every breath slow and even. At the bottom of the stairs, the air is oddly fresh, like it's seeping up from some underground fissure. He moves through the alley, past windows that have been bricked up for half a century. He can no longer see the figure, but there is only one way his quarry could have gone. A rodent scurries in his path. He stops, pauses for a moment, then continues. At the mouth of the alley he waits in the shadows and looks out.

If the prison itself is the top of the island, and the parade grounds and living quarters the middle, then this place is the absolute bottom of the island. The coastline and the docks, at sea level with the bay. Chip catches sight of the figure hustling south, toward the rocky shoals at the island's tip—almost directly below the cottages. Even in the bad light, he's certain: His quarry is carrying the stolen raincoats.

Chip looks left and right. There's no one else around. The boat is somewhere out on the water between the island and the city pier. He slips out along the path, sticking close to the dense foliage of the slope to his right. Rain clings to his face in a wet mask. He moves around the bend along a narrow strip of forbidding coastline: a joke of a beach, full of small rocks and crud washed up from the bay. He watches the figure halt in the shelter of a spindly tree, so gray and ashen that it appears to be hewn from the rocks. The figure sets the coats down at the water's edge. Then he kneels and produces a long plastic tube. Chip ducks behind some brush to watch, enthralled. His heart pounds.

The figure turns his head. His face, once hidden by the high collar of a dark trenchcoat, hits Chip like a flashbulb.

The high forehead. The hooded eyes. The shock of red hair beneath the peaked cap.

Eddie Thompson.

Benny and Maddie's father.

CHAPTER

The rain picks up. Chip keeps his head down. He's reeling with excitement and bursting with questions. He pushes them aside to stay in the moment. It's important to see exactly what Mr. Thompson is doing. He can digest it all later, back at the cottage.

The raincoats float in the shallows like a pool of melted yellow and blue. The plastic tube sticks up from the flat rubber. Chip watches as Mr. Thompson grips the tube and places the end in his mouth. His cheeks puff up like a blowfish's. He goes very still, intent on pushing air down into the tube, and pauses for a deep breath every few puffs.

To Chip's astonishment, the raincoats begin to rise like dough in an oven. He blinks at the unlikely sight, feeling like he must have dozed off in front of the TV. But he knows he's not dreaming. He wipes his wet face on the sleeve of his jacket. Mr. Thompson takes a huge breath and gives the raincoat blob one final puff. From Chip's hiding place, it's hard to tell how the whole contraption works. But the result is clear: The raincoats are inflated like balloons, bobbing in the water that laps against the rocks. He figures they must be stitched together somehow, but he isn't close enough to make out the seams.

Mr. Thompson lowers the tube, stands up, and gives the raincoat blob a gentle nudge. It moves like a small inflatable raft through the shallows. Mr. Thompson is careful not to let it get swept out into the bay. As he guides the raincoat raft slowly around the curve of the island, he moves out of sight.

"Rats," Chip mutters. This might be his only chance to witness something so vital to the case. He decides to risk tailing Mr. Thompson around the bend.

He leaves the shelter of the tree and works his way through the brush at the base of the slope. If he were to climb up through the scraggly foliage, he would reach the tip of the parade ground and the deputy warden's residence. He moves through a fog bank drifting in from the bay. A gray curtain descends. The shoreline vanishes. Fog clings to his jacket like a ghostly shroud. Mr. Thompson comes in and out of view. Chip extends a hand to make sure the coarse scrub is still off to his right. He swipes empty air.

Chip stops moving. For a dizzying moment, it's as if he's suspended in a cloud. The world as he knows it, with its rocks and lonely afternoons, is a distant and half-remembered thing. He is used to the fog on Alcatraz Island—it's part of the landscape, no different from the gulls and the lighthouse—but this is something else. This fog has a hissing, uncanny presence: a malevolent force, summoned to cover up illicit activities. He knows it's a crazy notion, that his mind is spinning out of control, but Chip feels like the fog is doing Mr. Thompson's bidding. Maddie's father is keeping secrets and the fog is his partner in crime.

Chip takes a breath and steadies his heartbeat. He sidesteps to the right. The edge of the slope should be *right here*. He doesn't understand how he's strayed so far. He listens for Mr. Thompson's footsteps, for the sloshing of the raincoat raft in the water. The foghorn's low bellow is all he can hear. He takes another step.

Abruptly, the foghorn cuts out. The warning system switches to the horn on the north side of the island. The two horns alternate in thirty-second intervals.

At the same time, his foot catches on a root. He stumbles, pitching forward, and cries out as he loses his balance completely.

Stupid.

It's a split-second sound, a quick little yelp. His knee comes down hard on a rock and he clamps his mouth shut to keep from making it worse. Motionless on his hands and knees, he waits.

"Who's there?" Mr. Thompson calls out after a moment. His voice sounds fearful and hollow in the sightless void.

Chip hears footsteps in the tiny rocks at the water's edge. If he stays here, Mr. Thompson will stumble right into him. On the other hand, if he moves, it will surely give away his position.

He waits until the dim shape of a man begins to emerge. His thoughts race. Mr. Thompson already knows *someone* is down here with him, but he doesn't know who it is. If Chip turns his back now, and puts as much of the fog bank between them as he can before he hits the dungeon alley—

He gathers his courage until he sees the shock of red hair appear out of the gray soup. Then he scrambles up off the rocks and runs back the way he came.

"Hey!" Mr. Thompson yells after him. "Stop!"

At least now Chip doesn't have to try to be quiet. He pumps his arms and lifts his knees. The fog drifts in patches and the world flashes by in bursts of clarity. Gravel, rocks, trees. The orange hull of a shipping vessel. Knots of seaweed and green slime. He can hear Mr. Thompson breathing hard at his back. A troubling question hits him: What will Mr. Thompson do to keep his secret safe—whatever this secret is?

Chip doesn't want to find out.

Other questions fire off in his mind. What does Benny know? What does *Maddie* know?

Why did she get him involved?

And why did she steer him toward Albert?

The mouth of the dungeon alley is a grim, stony maw, just ahead. He skids into the dim tunnel, his footsteps echoing down through the last century. How many others have fled through here? Frantic military guardsmen, prisoners infected with some kind of nineteenth-century madness. There is no place on this island that has not been traversed by those who came before. It's too small for new beginnings. Too small for almost everything. If Mr. Thompson catches him, there will be no avoiding him by blending in with the crowd.

Blood pounds in his ears. He hits the staircase at the end of the damp alley. Behind him, the heavy soles of Mr. Thompson's boots echo sharply off the old brick.

"Stop!" the man calls again. Chip's heart sinks as he leaps up the stairs two at a time. Is Mr. Thompson close enough to make out who he is? At the top of the stairs he takes a hard right toward the social hall, away from the parade ground and the residences. He can't risk leading Mr. Thompson right to his cottage.

The foghorn switches back to the south end. Chip slows his pace to a brisk walk. He takes off his jacket and folds it under his arm and doesn't look back. Inside the social hall, he heads for the counter at the soda fountain. A few other kids are there. He gives them a nod and takes an empty seat. Guards work the soda fountain in rotating shifts on weekends—today it's Mr. Fuller, a young bachelor who lives in one of the apartments across the parade ground from the cottages. Chip orders a root beer float, plants his elbows on the counter, and tries to look like he's been there all day. Mr. Fuller leans into the cooler and comes up with a massive scoop of vanilla ice cream. Ray Charles is on the record player.

Behind him, the door opens and shuts. A man, breathing hard, stomps into the hall. Chip thinks he should have gone straight to the bowling alley on the first floor, but there really wasn't time. He hunches over the counter, keeping his back turned, as Mr. Fuller slides him the root beer float. A spoon handle and a thick straw striped like a barber pole stick up from the glass.

"Hey there, Eddie," Mr. Fuller says, greeting Mr. Thompson.

Stillness. Chip imagines Mr. Thompson surveying the room. Eyes down, he sips his drink. The door opens and shuts again. Chip glances over his shoulder. Mr. Thompson is gone. He exhales, lets his body relax.

"Old Eddie looked a little lost," Mr. Fuller says with a grin. Then he busies himself drying glasses with a rag. "Raining out there?" he says idly. It takes Chip a moment to realize Mr. Fuller is talking to him.

"Oh," Chip says. "Yeah."

"You look like a drowned rat, kid." Mr. Fuller turns to wipe down the milkshake machine. Chip's hand goes to his hair. It's soaked, plastered to his head. He glances down the counter. The other kids are perfectly dry. Even from the back, from where Mr. Thompson was standing a moment ago, Chip's shiny, wet hair would stick out. There might as well be flashing lights above his head with a big red arrow pointing down at him.

He wonders if all is lost. If Eddie Thompson now knows exactly who was spying on his little trip to the water's edge with his kids' stitched-together raincoats.

Chip turns the image over in his mind: Mr. Thompson inflating the makeshift raft, nudging it along the shallows. Testing it. Seeing if it's seaworthy. He devours the big scoop of ice cream. Then he drains the root beer. Outside, rain slashes down through the fog like tiny silver bullets.

Chip taps the side of his empty glass. "Keep 'em coming, Mr. Fuller."

The young guard raises an eyebrow.

"Um," Chip says, "please."

CHAPTER

The first knock on the cottage door comes at eight o'clock. Chip goes to answer but his father beats him to it. Dressed in rumpled slacks and an old work shirt, his father is the picture of comfort on a day off from his duties at the prison. Chip stands at the other end of the hall while his father welcomes Mrs. Harrison out of the misty night. Their next-door neighbor shrugs off Chip's father's offer to take her coat. Through some grown-up-lady magic, she spins out of her shawl and removes her overcoat without setting down her handbag.

She spots Chip and gives him a smile. "I heard my two eldest gave you and the McCain boy a drubbing at the lanes." Chip tries to smile back. He'd teamed up with Albert after all, and it hadn't been much fun. "No hard feelings, I hope."

She tosses her coat over the banister.

"He's looking forward to a rematch!" Chip's father says with a too-big grin. Chip recalls the happy look on his father's face when he'd spotted his son bowling at the social hall. It's a complicated feeling, knowing his father is relieved to see Chip playing with the other kids on the island while at the same time knowing it doesn't mean they're his friends. He wonders what his father would say if he knew Chip was only bowling because Albert strong-armed him into it.

"Sure am," Chip agrees.

Chip's father ushers Mrs. Harrison down the hall. On the way, she taps the newspaper, smack in the middle of Robert Kennedy's face. "With the way our esteemed attorney general is cracking down on the mob, I do believe you'll be guarding some new guests very soon."

His father's expression falters. "I don't know where we'll put them all."

Mrs. Harrison gestures into the air. "Perhaps you could make room for them here. What do you say, Chip—want to host a few Chicago gangsters?"

She mimics firing a tommy-gun at the wall, then joins his father in the living room. Chip lifts a toothpick to his mouth and imagines a half-dozen ruthless criminals lining up with their plates, waiting for Chip to dish out reheated swordfish and green beans.

The second knock at the door comes a moment later. Before Chip or his father can answer it, the door flies open and Albert's father, Declan McCain, strides into the front hall.

"Who's ready to lose their shirt?" he calls out. Mr. McCain's bald head glints in the hanging lamp Chip's mother had picked out when they first moved in. He sheds the coat from his massive frame and tosses it to Chip without a word. Chip swims in the fabric. It smells like cheap cologne. He hangs the coat in the closet.

"June!" Mr. McCain greets Mrs. Harrison in the living room. "Shouldn't you be home with your brood?"

Chip hears the soft clink of ice in glasses.

"No, Declan—they'll cope just fine without me for an evening. Shouldn't you be bailing your son out of the county jail for some petty, idiotic infraction?"

Mr. McCain laughs in a loud, fake way that makes Chip's face hurt, like he's just chomped down on tinfoil. "Albert can't help it if he's more of a man at thirteen than your Kenneth is at fifteen."

"And I'm sure that kind of *man* is exactly what Kenneth aspires to be."

"Yeah?" Mr. McCain says. "What kind is that?"

"All right, all right," his father's voice cuts in. "The game tonight is called Texas Hold'em. It's all the rage in Vegas."

"What's wrong with regular poker?" Mr. McCain says.

"It's merely a variation," Mrs. Harrison says.

"You'll pick it up fast," Chip's father says. "As soon as—"

There's a polite knock on the door, two quick raps.

"Chip!" his father calls out.

Chip opens the door. Eddie Thompson stands before him, looking much different from the man he'd seen skulking around the shore in the rain. Now Benny and Maddie's father is decked out in a tan suit and coat with plaid lapels and sleeves. A fedora's perched on his head at a jaunty angle. His red hair is tamed and slicked back with Brylcreem.

Chip blinks. Mr. Thompson smiles. The gleam in his eyes hints at buried meaning. Chip tells himself to act like nothing's out of the ordinary. He's greeting the guests at his father's monthly poker night. No big deal.

"Hi, Mr. Thompson," he says, stepping aside so the man can enter the house.

"What's the good word, Chip?" He transfers his fedora to the hat rack jutting from the wall just inside the door. Then he takes off his coat and hands it over.

"Same old, same old," Chip says, hanging Mr. Thompson's coat in the closet.

"Rain's letting up," the man says, smoothing his hair where the hatband dug furrows. "It was a dreary afternoon." He pauses in an exaggerated thinking pose. "Come to think of it, yesterday was dreary, too. And the day before that." He looks puzzled. "Remind me—why do we live on this godforsaken rock again?"

"I don't have a choice," Chip says.

Mr. Thompson considers this. "You know, Chip—I always say this to Maddie and Benny: You're going to be in for a rude awakening when you get a little older and realize that none of us grown-ups have as many choices as you think we do, either."

"I'm not going to choose to live *here*, though," he says.

"And where are you going to live?"

"San Francisco." He pauses. "Or maybe Chicago. Or New

York." He's never really thought about living so far away before—all the way across the country—but it sounds exciting when he says it out loud. After all, the skyscrapers get taller the farther east you go.

Mr. Thompson pretends to be surprised. "You don't want to be an Alcatraz guard like your old man? It's a noble profession. Somebody's gotta make sure the incorrigibles don't run roughshod over everyday people."

"I don't know what I want to be," he lies.

Mr. Thompson frowns and crosses his arms over his chest. "That's not what I heard. Word on the street is, you're going to be a real-life Jake Hall. Chip Carter, private investigator."

Chip doesn't say a word. Inside, he once again curses this island where everyone knows everything about everyone else.

"In fact," Mr. Thompson continues, "scuttlebutt says you've already got a little head start on the competition. Playing detective from one end of our fair island to the other."

I'm not playing, he wishes he had the guts to say. *And you're hiding something big.*

Mr. Thompson leans toward Chip and lowers his voice. "Listen, Chip. What happened on last week's *Hall of Justice* episode?"

Chip wonders where the man is going with this. "Jake got mixed up in that business with the racetrack. Using carrier pigeons to fix the races."

"Right. On the surface. But what was *really* going on was—"

"The mayor was going to lose the election, so he was framing the guy running against him, and he almost got away with it, until Jake asked his ex-girlfriend Esmeralda to help him with the bird angle, and she figured out that the mayor's grandfather was this champion pigeon breeder back in the day, which nobody knew because he was adopted, but—"

"Right," Mr. Thompson says, a little taken aback. "Good memory. But what was the big reveal?"

"The mayor knew the guy who was going to beat him was bad. The guy was corrupt, in the pocket of these criminals, and even though the mayor had to break the law to win the election, Jake let him get away with it in the end."

"Because the other guy was *worse*," Mr. Thompson says, like he's imparting great wisdom.

"I know," Chip says. "I watched the episode."

"Eddie!" Chip's father calls from the living room. "Get in here so I can deal everybody in."

"Before my clothes go out of style!" Mr. McCain says.

"Unless we can all be transported back to 1948," says Mrs. Harrison, "I'm afraid that ship has long since left the harbor."

Mr. Thompson straightens up and buttons his sport coat. "All I'm saying, Chip, is that a good detective changes how he ought to think about the entire case when he finds out things aren't quite what they seem."

"So how *are* things, then, Mr. Thompson?"

The man appears startled for a moment. Chip can't believe what he just blurted out.

Mr. Thompson's face darkens. "I'm going to play cards now," he says, and heads into the living room.

Chip peeks in. His father has shoved two armchairs back

to make room for the card table with its green felt surface. He pours a bag of potato chips into a silver bowl. Chip watches the players take their seats around the table. Mr. Thompson laces his fingers together and stretches his arms. His knuckles crack. Mrs. Harrison's gaze lingers on the wooden birds frozen in flight across the wall. Chip's mother used to call them her flock. Mrs. Harrison reaches out and lays a hand lightly on one of the birds. She pulls her hand away and examines the dust on her finger. Then she catches Chip's eye and smiles ruefully, as if she's been caught in the act.

CHAPTER

The clock strikes midnight. Chip, pajama clad and barefoot, kneels down in the corner of the spare room. Boxes full of his mother's clothes are piled on a sofa shoved against the wall. A dresser full of sewing needles, thread, and bits of fabric sits in the corner. Behind him, the heavy bag hangs from a chain.

He bends his ear to a vent in the floor. Voices from the living room rise up like smoke. The words sound thin and hollow, but easy enough to make out. This late, there are only two people left at the card table: Chip's father and Mr. Thompson.

"Declan needs to watch his mouth," Mr. Thompson says. He sounds steamed. Mr. McCain left a half hour ago, but Mr. Thompson is still going on about the man.

"Cut him some slack, Eddie," Chip's father says. "He's having a tough go of it."

Chip files this away. He doesn't know anything about Albert McCain's family life. A thrill courses through him. The warm rush of information he's not supposed to hear. Secrets: the private detective's currency. His bread and butter.

"Is that why you insist on inviting him every month? Some kind of charity work you're doing?"

"That's not fair." There is the papery flutter of a deck being cut and shuffled. Chip has seen the way his father bends two stacks of cards between his thumbs and knuckles and lets them cascade down together into one deck.

Mr. Thompson sighs. "I know, I know." He chuckles softly. "June really winds him up. It's a sight to behold."

"She oughta be in pictures."

"Missed her calling, all right."

A long moment of silence hangs between them. Someone crunches potato chips. This time, when Chip's father speaks, his voice is even lower. Chip lies down on the hardwood floor and presses his ear to the cool metal grate of the vent.

"How'd it go today?"

"Magnificent. I gotta hand it to you, Hiram—the plastic tube's a stroke of genius. Maybe you missed your calling, too."

"Yeah, well, *raft engineer* wasn't exactly an option when I got out of the service."

The warm rush of secret information turns ice-cold. Chip feels like he's frozen to the floor. A shameful part of him wants to lift his ear from the vent, tiptoe back to bed where he can't hear a thing, shut his eyes tight, and wait for sleep to claim him. Then tomorrow he can tell himself it was all a dream.

No way his father could be involved in whatever secret business Eddie Thompson's getting up to.

He remembers the plastic tube, Eddie's puffed-up cheeks. The stitched-together raincoats slowly inflating. The odd little raft bobbing in the water.

"Anyway," Mr. Thompson says, affecting a pirate voice, "'twas a fine seaworthy craft."

"So it floated."

"Passed both my test runs. And today it inflated easy as a balloon."

Chip's father exhales loudly. Chip can sense his relief. "Does he know?"

He, Chip thinks. *He who?*

"Not yet. Monday's my day off. I'm meeting one of his lackeys in the city."

"Sciortino?"

Mr. Thompson laughs. "Nobody with that much juice. Some mug they call Zipper, hangs out in the back of the Silver Spoon. I'll give him the lowdown then. I'll be sure to tell him your idea's aces."

"This is big, Eddie. This is real progress."

"It's good news, sure." Mr. Thompson sounds cautious. "But it's not like Jimmy the Hat's in the good news business. I don't see him letting off the squeeze even a little bit till we see this all the way through."

Chip goes even colder. Everybody in San Francisco knows

who Jimmy the Hat is: James Lanza, boss of the San Francisco crime family. Some mafia dons keep it hush-hush, stay out of the spotlight, conduct business from the shadows. Not Jimmy the Hat. He's in all the papers. Every kid on Alcatraz knows about Jimmy.

His father mutters something he can't quite hear.

"Nobody's going to find out," Mr. Thompson says. "Not if we keep it buttoned up. The Hat isn't interested in exposing us—that defeats the whole purpose. It's all supposed to come from the inside."

"I'll sleep better when it's done, is all."

"That makes two of us."

There's the sound of a chair scraping on the living room floor as Mr. Thompson rises from the table. "One last thing, Hiram—seems your boy's becoming quite the little detective."

His father chuckles. "He never misses *Hall of Justice*, I'll tell you that much."

There's a pause that Chip reads as awkward. He reaches for a toothpick, but the little box is back in his bedroom. *This is it,* he thinks. *The moment Mr. Thompson rats me out.*

Footsteps echo. Someone rummages in the hall closet. The men are too far from the living room vent. Their voices are muffled. Chip holds his breath as the front door opens and closes. He listens to his father puttering around the living room, cleaning up.

Then Chip pads quietly down the hall to his bedroom. Earlier, he knew what would happen if he were to get caught creeping around after bedtime. A very light scolding, the offer of a glass of water, a half-serious command to get back to bed.

Now it's as if the floor is made of a less forgiving sub-stance. The house somehow creakier. And his father? An unknown presence. A man in league with Eddie Thompson, involved in whatever he's doing with those raincoats. And with Jimmy the Hat!

Downstairs, his father moves the armchairs back into place.

In his room, Chip climbs into bed and takes his notebook and little silver penlight from his nightstand. While it's fresh in his mind, Chip records his father's conversation with Mr. Thompson. When he's done, he reads it over again.

In *Hall of Justice*, the scenes where Jake Hall is going back over his notes, feet propped on his messy desk, are accompanied by tense, burbling music. There's always a close-up shot of the detective's furrowed brow. When the puzzle pieces fall into place, the music swells. Jake's eyes widen. He leaps from his chair, papers exploding off the desk like birds taking flight, snatches up his jacket and hat, and rushes from the office. Cut to commercial.

But all Chip sees are words in his chicken-scratch scrawl. There's no violin sawing madly, no cello hitting ominous notes. No magic moment when everything falls into place. Just the sound of his father coming up the stairs. Chip flicks his light off, shoves his notebook under his pillow, and shuts his eyes.

His father comes down the hall. The footsteps stop. Chip doesn't have to open his eyes to know that his father is peering into his bedroom, checking on him. Chip tells himself that it's really no different at all—if he hadn't been listening at the vent in the spare room, everything would be the same as the night before, and the night before that. But what kind of detective wishes to go back and un-hear the secrets that might crack the case? He has to face the truth. Even if it's uncomfortable. Even if it hits too close to home.

Chip knows all this is true. And yet, what he really wants, deep in his heart, is for his father to come into his room, kneel down at his bedside, and tell him everything's fine, there's a perfectly innocent explanation. It's just grown-up stuff that Chip doesn't understand.

In this moment he *wants* to be left in the dark. Just another kid fumbling his way through life on the island. Right now, he would give up his whole future in the big city, his name on the glass door, for a second chance at a normal life with his mother and father.

But this is a useless desire, as empty as the prisoner up on the hill wishing to wake up and find that his cell door has opened to the outside world. That he is suddenly, magically, free.

His father moves down the hall. Chip opens his eyes and gazes into the darkness. And just like that, he understands. It's in Mr. Thompson's words: *It's supposed to come from the inside.*

Chip is sure that *inside* can only mean one thing.

The prison on the hill. Steel bars and lockdowns and yard brawls. The fog slipping in through gaps in the old concrete, unfurling like an endless cape along the scuffed floor of the cellblock where his father's heavy boots keep time . . .

CHAPTER

INSIDE

Another day at Alcatraz has come and gone and now the Watcher is back in his cell. At 9:30 the lights-out count kicks off; a few minutes later it is finished. The cell goes dark. The guard's footsteps echo down the block. The Watcher waits a moment for his eyes to adjust. The simple contents of his cell take on a shadowy quality: washbasin, cot, toilet, shelf, books, accordion case.

Moving in near darkness, he retrieves his digging tool from the center of a hollowed-out book: a nail file welded with bits of melted silver to a spoon handle. It is a tool of the Watcher's invention, crafted after some trial and error from scraped bits of dimes and the heat of fifty matches. Each of the four men has one. He goes to the rear of his cell and, with one last glance over his shoulder at the empty corridor, quietly slides the accordion case away from the cement wall.

The metal grille of the vent appears. Through its grate is the darkness of the corridor behind the cells. He turns his peacoat inside out and lays it along the floor beneath the grille to muffle the noise should a big chunk of wall suddenly fall out. He runs his makeshift pick in the groove in the side of the metal grille. He finds the indentation he has been painstakingly working on for the past few nights. Then he begins chipping away. Dust and jagged little pieces of plaster pile up on the fabric of his coat. Tomorrow he will pocket the rubble and ditch it out in the yard. He must fight the urge to dig like a madman. He can remove only whatever plaster he can fit in his pocket. Every action creates more problems to solve. His pockets must not bulge or he will attract attention.

The Watcher does not mind. Slow is better.

The problem is, he knows that Jimmy the Hat—the crime boss on the outside who pulls the strings—is not a patient man. Holding court in the back of his social club, the gangster is accustomed to snapping his fingers and making things happen. From what little information the Watcher has gleaned from Red, Jimmy the Hat is going to deal the prison its death blow.

Their escape will be part of this. There are other parts, too, but he does not know what they are. He does not care. They do not concern him.

The Watcher moves the spoon handle back and forth. Bits of

plaster dust rain down from the groove. It is interesting, being used as a tool—the same way he is using the modified spoon. He will never meet Jimmy the Hat. If the plan succeeds, the Watcher will hightail it far from San Francisco, never to return. And if it should fail, he will likely wind up with a belt around his neck, hanging from a pipe in the shop, or a shank in the guts. The Watcher wonders idly if Jimmy the Hat will use Red for the task of silencing him forever. The Watcher decides the mobster will probably use the other guard on his payroll—what's his name. Carter. Hiram Carter. That one is a real bruiser. They say he used to be a top amateur boxer, maybe could have even turned pro.

The Watcher has never received a direct threat from Jimmy the Hat through his two crooked guards. He just assumes that if the plot fails, the gangster will not want to leave any loose ends.

However it all ends up, it is worth it to the Watcher. He is not sure if the Anglins and West feel the same. For them, the notion of freedom is the shining beacon on the hill. They are the type of men who listen wistfully as the sounds of the tourist boats drift across the island. The laughter and conversation of people who have never known what it is like to be confined within cement and steel cages. They listen and long to be the people on those boats.

The Watcher smiles inwardly as he scrapes away tiny bits of plaster while the rest of the prisoners bed down for the night. For him, the world beyond the prison does not really matter. It has never given him much of a fair shake, after all. It is no shining beacon, just another place.

The real freedom is in the escape itself. Waiting. Watching. Figuring out the angles.

Beating the system.

Suddenly, his digger punches hard through the wall. His arm jolts forward. The tool is all the way through. Startled, the Watcher takes a moment to gather his thoughts. He wiggles the handle. Bits of plaster and crumbs of cement fall from the hole. He widens the opening. The wall is thick but there are old, soft patches that surround the metal grille. He has just hit one. Like a gold prospector hitting a rich vein, a sense of satisfaction washes over him.

It has been a good day. The raft is going to work. John Anglin will bring up the cheap plastic raincoats one by one from the stockpile in the basement. He calculates that they will need at least fifty. And soon, very soon, he will be able to explore the shaft beyond the wall and chart their course to the roof of the prison.

He sends a silent plea to Jimmy the Hat: Sit tight. It will not be long now.

The *Warden Johnston* pitches against the chop. Swells slap the sides of the boat. In his office in the cabin's back row, Chip smells salt and ageless depths. He slides a toothpick deftly from one side of his mouth to the other, keeping silent watch. Up front, Mr. Thompson sits and chats with his son, Benny. Chip can see only the back of Benny's head, but he can feel the boy's anxious vibrations from ten rows back. Maddie's here, too; she's just not the kind of kid who sits with her father on the way to school.

Chip doesn't know what kind of kid he'd be in the same situation. His own father rarely leaves the island.

The deep thwacks of leather gloves on the rough canvas punching bag echo in the back of his mind. Last night his father was up late throwing punch after punch, timing as even as a metronome. He closes his eyes. *THWACK. THWACK.* Nothing drowns it out.

Monday mornings are quiet aboard the boat. Another weekend come and gone, every kid staring down the barrel of another five-day stretch of school. Chip glances to the side. He's alone in the back row, as usual. He leans over and unzips his backpack. For the tenth time today, he takes inventory. Satisfied that all his gear is in place, he sits back and returns his gaze to the window.

An early tour boat chugs away from Fisherman's Wharf. Small figures move across the pier. The gray sky hangs low over the city, draping fog across the skyline. The *Warden Johnston* slows as it approaches its docking site. Chip takes one last look out until he sees it. The white spire crowning Telegraph Hill: Coit Tower, its concrete tip vanishing in the haze. Just down the hill from the tower is the Silver Spoon Diner, where Mr. Thompson is supposed to meet with Zipper, Jimmy the Hat's messenger boy.

Chip is grateful that his eavesdropping gave up this tidbit of information. Now he doesn't have to follow Mr. Thompson too closely through the streets and risk getting caught. He knows where the man is going.

The boat bumps lightly against the slick posts that rise up along the pier. The passengers shoulder their schoolbags and crowd the aisle, waiting to file off. Halfway up, Roger Pettys hands Albert a sheet of paper crowded with neat writing: math homework. Fractions and quadratic equations. Albert takes a crumpled sheet from his backpack and compares the two. Everyone files toward the exit. Albert scribbles furiously. Chip brings up the rear. The floor of the boat rolls with the swells. He flicks his toothpick into the trash on the way out. Composes his face into a bored Monday Morning Look to match his schoolmates.

He watches the ancient crewman, Mr. Callahan, lower the gangplank from the side of the boat down to the pier. Mr. Thompson claps the old white-haired man on the back as he steps off the boat. Chip watches through the window as Mr. Thompson bids his son goodbye, thrusts his hands into the pockets of his trenchcoat, and takes off walking toward the busy Embarcadero, the four-lane street that runs along the waterfront at the northeastern bend of the city, from the Bay Bridge to the tip of Russian Hill.

Chip shuffles up the aisle and out onto the deck. It's one of those spring days in San Francisco that seems plucked from another season entirely. Is there a hint of summer in the air or winter on the wind coming in across the bay? Nobody can be sure. His footsteps clang on the metal gangplank. Mr. Callahan gives him a sleepy nod.

Off the boat, in the city, the line of kids dissolves into cliques. Albert flicks Roger's ear with his meaty finger. Roger shoves him back hard. They go at it on the sidewalk, a mock fight teetering on the edge of chaos. The Harrison kids race past them. Mary and Kenneth split off to hassle Albert as he hooks an arm around Roger's neck. Half the Alcatraz kids weave through early morning tourists on the pier like dogs off their leashes. The other half plod along, dragging Monday blues with them off the boat.

Their school is a few blocks away, along the southward curve of Embarcadero. Chip slows his pace. He watches carefully to account for every kid from the boat. His eyes dart across their backs as they get smaller. A cable car slides into the Sansome Street stop. The wind kicks up. Chip stops walking. Nobody turns around to see if he's still there. He figures nobody cares. It won't be until Mr. Franconi takes roll that his absence will be noted. Then it will be reported to the main office. At some point in the morning, a secretary will get around to calling his house. Nobody will answer—his father will be at work. More time will go by as a message is passed up to the prison. Eventually, when he gets a break, his father will call the school.

Chip has no plan for what happens after that.

Jake Hall goes where the investigation leads him. There are always consequences. You just have to deal with them.

But that's later.

Now Chip waits for the traffic lights to turn red. When the cars stop, he crosses the road. He notes the makes and models of the boxy sedans, the fresh produce trucks, the Volkswagens with their rounded hoods and headlights like eyes. He's training his mind to home in on details.

On the other side of Embarcadero, he starts up the hill toward the Silver Spoon Diner. His backpack makes him self-conscious. He looks exactly like a kid playing hooky. There are truant officers in the city, their sole job to hunt for kids skipping school. He figures they're mostly busting older kids in the Tenderloin, not twelve-year-olds on Telegraph Hill. It's unfair, but so is everything else in the big city. And if the unfairness tilts in his favor to help him work this case, then he'll take what he can get.

A surge of excitement courses through him. The world sharpens. His senses drink in the city as if all the pores on his skin have been opened at once. A little brown corgi on a pink leash stares up at him with a smile. Halfway up the hill, a million city scents wash over him, gasoline and grime and food cooked over an open flame. The day will come when there will be no school to skip. When this will simply be his life. Chip Carter, San Francisco's greatest—

"Hey, Chip!"

The voice comes from behind him. Stunned, he freezes. Who could possibly know he's here?

He turns. Maddie Thompson stands there grinning. "Where are we going?"

"Nowhere," Chip says.

She fixes him with a skeptical look. "Well, *somewhere*. Obviously."

"Nowhere important."

"Somewhere that's not school." She pauses. "I'm coming with you."

"Buzz off, Maddie. I work alone."

Her eyes light up. "So it's connected to the case."

"Maybe it's a different case."

"Yeah? How many you working?"

He turns his back and walks up the hill. A moment later she's at his side.

"I'm just going for a root beer float," he says.

"It's eight in the morning."

"I got a bad craving. You go back now, you can still make it to school before the morning bell."

A woman pushes a stroller out a coffee shop. The baby, swaddled in blankets, tosses a stuffed elephant onto the sidewalk. Without breaking his stride, Chip scoops it up and tosses it back.

"I want to know how the investigation is going," Maddie says. "I hired you. You owe me that much."

Chip stops walking. He turns to Maddie. He knows he should bite his tongue and focus on the task at hand, but he can't help himself. It isn't just Mr. Thompson who's striking a bum note here. There was Benny's attempt to get him to drop the case, mere hours after he got wise to it even existing at all. Then there was Maddie herself, kicking the whole thing off by pointing him right at Albert McCain.

Something's fishy with every last one of these Thompsons.

"All right, Maddie. I've got some good news and some bad news about the raincoats."

"Bad news first."

He thinks of the raincoats joined together by some kind of glue or stitching, inflated with a tube, bobbing at the water's edge. "You're not getting them back."

"What's the good news?"

"You knew that already, so it won't be much of a shock."

Maddie looks startled. "I don't know what you're talking about."

"Sure you do. You and Benny both."

"Benny? What's he got to do with this?"

Chip doesn't know, not exactly. He's letting his mouth run away faster than his brain. Poking at things he's only beginning to understand. "Why don't you tell me?"

"You flipped your lid or something? Tell you *what*?"

"How's this: You put me onto Albert McCain to throw me off the scent from day one. Albert doesn't have anything to do with this and you know it."

Her face reddens. "I don't know anything."

Chip loses his patience. "Sure. Now listen. I'm going to find out what your father's doing meeting one of Jimmy the Hat's errand boys in the Silver Spoon." He thinks of Mr. Thompson and his father sitting at the poker table late into the night.

It's supposed to come from the inside.

I'll sleep better when it's done.

He leaves that part out for now. Chip and Maddie are like rocks in a stream as the morning rush of the city moves past them. Commuters in hats head downhill, briefcases clutched at their sides. He lets his words sink in as he studies Maddie's face. She doesn't say anything. She doesn't have to. He reads the fear in her eyes. The mask falls away. Without a word, she takes back her denials.

"Jimmy the Hat?" she says. "My dad's involved with gangsters?"

My dad, too, Chip thinks. He pops a toothpick in his mouth. He waits for the wheels in Maddie's head to quit spinning. He's surprised by the anger in her eyes as she starts spilling her guts.

"It all started a few weeks ago." She pauses, gathering her words. "I never thought about what kind of person my dad was before, because he was always just *my dad*, you know? But then something changed. He didn't laugh as much. He got super serious all the time. And he got a temper." She pauses and looks away. "He's never really yelled at Benny and me before, but lately, we can't do anything right. It's like that movie *Invasion of the Body Snatchers*. Like he's been taken over by somebody different, who looks just like him." She looks at Chip for a long time. "My mom is really sad. None of us can understand." She swallows, composes herself. "And those darn raincoats. One day he just comes home with them, out of the blue. Then a few days later, they were gone. Like he gave 'em to us, but then he changed his mind. That was the last straw."

"That was when you hired me."

"Yeah." She shuffles her feet, kicks a pebble off the curb. "I know it was wrong to blame Albert. But I thought . . ." She looks at an overflowing garbage can next to a cement stoop. "I don't know what I thought."

Chip reels in his sharp tone, makes his voice gentle. "Why didn't you just tell me the truth from the start? I could have started looking into your dad right away, instead of . . . bowling with Albert."

She laughs, bitter as a radish. "Maybe I wanted it to be something simple, some stupid prank Albert did, not my dad hiding something."

Chip frowns, lost in thought. "But you wanted me to find the truth."

"I wanted both things, all right?" Now she sounds mad at *him*. He looks at this girl, her dark hair falling in a loose bob around her ears, her eyes fierce in a way he's never seen before. *Both things.* His mind spins. Maddie Thompson wanted him to find out what was going on inside her family, and at the same time she wanted that thing to be *nothing at all*. Yet she must have known that it would not be nothing. Chip's mind stretches toward understanding. It's amazing, what we can hold in our heads.

Maddie didn't lie to him. Not exactly. She simply had a wish and tried to make it come true. Even though she knew it probably would not.

For some reason, it all brings to mind his father, pummeling the heavy bag so hard that the flock of wooden birds on the living room wall trembles. His father, who took one look at his son bowling with Albert McCain and the older kids next door and practically beamed. His father, who thinks his son will be taking a friend to a baseball game sometime soon.

"Okay," Chip says.

"Okay what?"

"Come with me."

CHAPTER

12

The sign outside the Silver Spoon Diner says QUALITY FOOD FAMILY OWNED. A big picture of a smiling hamburger hangs in one of the windows. From across the street, Chip can see that it's bustling with the breakfast crowd. He can just barely make out the soda fountain behind the counter. A root beer float would really calm his nerves.

Chip and Maddie duck into an alley, out of sight. A pile of empty milk crates leans against the wall. A too-sweet smell like fruit gone bad leaks from a trash bin whose lid hangs askew. Chip unslings his backpack and sets it down on the pavement.

"So this is what you do?" she asks, glancing around.

"Big-time," Chip says, even though this is his second case ever and his first non-cat-related mystery. "There's always an alley." He unzips the bag and pulls out the battered peaked cap he found in the back of the coat closet. It must have belonged to his father when he was younger. He pulls it down over his head. It's a size too big, but it will have to do. Next, he puts on a pair of glasses with thick black frames. There are no lenses in them. He's hoping no one will notice.

Maddie grins. "Do I get a disguise, too?"

"You get to keep watch out here. Be my eyes and ears. Any more of Jimmy the Hat's goons come close, you pound on the window of the diner and run."

She considers this. "How am I gonna know if it's a goon or just a regular guy who wants breakfast?"

"In this business, we gotta trust our gut, Maddie." He pulls up the collar on his jacket to brush against his chin.

"You look like you're starring in the school play," she says.

He ignores this. "One more thing. Benny came to my house the day you hired me. Tried to warn me off the case. At the time, I figured he was just scared of Albert."

Maddie sighs. She looks out the mouth of the alley, toward the diner. Her father isn't visible in any of the window seats. Chip figures he's in a booth in the back, behind the counter. "My brother's scared my parents are gonna split up," she says. "He doesn't want to know what's going on. He thinks I'm a meddler, that I'm making it worse. He thinks if we hide our heads in the sand, it'll all go away."

Chip zips his bag. "Maybe he's right."

Maddie fixes him with a look. "He's not."

"We could just let things play out. Live our lives. Ignore it all.

Hope it doesn't really change anything." He thinks of his father at the poker table. "What I'm saying is, once you start digging, you might uncover things you wish you hadn't." He pauses. "Say the word and we'll go back to school and forget all this."

"I thought you worked alone?"

He hands her the backpack. "So did I."

She slings it over her shoulder. "I guess you never really know somebody."

He turns toward the diner, one step closer to finding out what connects his father and Mr. Thompson to San Francisco's most powerful crime boss. He pulls the brim of his hat down low. A shadow falls across his face.

"Guess not," he agrees. A car horn drowns out the words.

CHAPTER

13

A bearded man in baggy clothes opens the door of the Silver Spoon. He thrusts out a dented cup. Chip fishes a dime from his pocket and drops it in. The man closes the door behind him. The smell of fried food and grease wafts from the kitchen. A white-hatted cook plunks a pair of big round plates down on the kitchen ledge and rings a bell. A waitress glides past, scoops up the plates, and delivers them to a pair of old ladies. A counterman clad in crisp whites pours coffee from a steaming pot.

"How many?" A middle-aged woman appears before him.

"I'm meeting somebody." Chip makes a show of looking around. Most of the booths are full. In the back, a narrow hall-way runs past the side of the counter and leads to the restroom.

It's lined with two-seater booths. He spots Eddie Thompson's red hair. A gaunt man in a fedora sits across from him, hunched like a bird of prey, sipping coffee. "Over there," he says vaguely. The woman hands him a menu and bustles off.

He moves slowly, taking in the scene. A stroke of luck: Mr. Thompson is sitting with his back to the door. He won't see the kid in the too-big hat and glasses coming down the row of booths.

The cook rings the bell. Another waitress swoops in. The counterman clears plates. A busboy wipes down a table with a rag. A little girl in pigtails stacks sugar packets.

He's close enough now to see that Mr. Thompson's booth is sandwiched between two empty ones. Rectangular glass partitions rise a few inches above the seat backs to divide them. He opts for the booth behind Mr. Thompson. That way he won't have to walk past him. The two men are talking in low voices. Chip keeps his eyes low and slides into the seat. He opens his menu, pretending to read. There's a radio on in the kitchen, the clatter of forks on plates, the low murmur of conversation. Chip leans back against the partition and focuses on the two men at his back. A high, reedy voice is easy to pick up on. The man in the fedora. Zipper.

"It ain't been all silk with you so far, Eddie. The Hat don't like to be strung along."

"Nobody's stringing anybody along," Mr. Thompson insists. "I told you, Hiram just cracked the raft problem." He pauses. "You made me meet you here for a report, there's your report."

"Don't get snippy with me. The guy passing your messages

to the Hat ain't the guy you want on your bad side."

Chip leaves his laminated menu open on the table. He figures nobody will bother him if it looks like he's still deciding. He figures wrong. Suddenly, a waitress is looming over him, snapping her gum. Her apron is spotless except for a single blemish that looks like an inked fingerprint. He waits for her to ask if he ought to be in school.

"Anything to drink?" is all she says. Behind him, Eddie Thompson says something he can't hear.

"Water, please," Chip says in as deep a voice as he can manage. He peers up through his fake glasses.

"Oh, I got all the big spenders today," the waitress says. Then she flashes a smile. "Just messin' with you, kid. Our finest water, coming up." She hurries away.

Chip picks up the conversation at his back.

"I'm serious," Zipper is saying, "you gotta try the egg cream. Best in the city."

"I don't like egg creams."

"Your loss."

"Listen, is there anything else?"

One of the men, probably Zipper, plunks down a mug. "You in a hurry to get back to your godforsaken rock?"

Chip can sense Mr. Thompson's discomfort in the long silence. "I just want to make sure we're square with the Hat for now and get out of here. No offense."

"None taken. Lemme ask you something, though, Eddie. Something I always wondered. That night at cards, why didn't you just quit while you were ahead? You and your old buddy, the pug."

A shiver comes over Chip. A pug is a pugilist—a boxer. Zipper's talking about his father. The waitress brings his water along with a straw. "You know what you want, kid?"

Chip, straining to hear the conversation in the booth behind him, orders so fast he almost forgets to use his deep voice. "Two eggs."

"How do you like 'em?"

"Scrambled."

"Home fries or toast?"

Chip considers the pair of quarters in his pocket. "Neither."

"You just want plain old eggs, that's it?"

"That's it."

She sighs and takes his menu. "Eggs and water it is, then." She studies him for a moment. "Nice glasses." Chip manages a weak smile. She walks away. He hears her say "Weird kid" under her breath. Then he leans back and listens in.

"You don't remember me, I bet," Zipper continues, "but I was working the room that night. Making sure nobody pulls a fast one at the Hat's poker game. Which I might add you'd have to be real foolish to try. That's how I saw the pug go all in and blow it." Zipper laughs. "He plays cards like a house on fire, don't he?"

"We both had a run of bad luck that night, is all."

"Yeah, well, I don't believe in luck, Eddie. And you oughta consider a healthy disbelief yourself, since luck don't seem to believe in you, either. Way I see it, you and the pug, you're getting off easy with this whole Alcatraz scheme. I seen the Hat do a lot worse to saps who owe him a lot less."

"I don't care how you see it. Are we done here?"

Chip can hear Mr. Thompson bristling at Zipper steering the conversation. At the same time, his mind works on overdrive. Pieces fall into place. He remembers one Saturday night back in February. His father had taken a rare trip into the city, and he didn't get home until nearly dawn—Chip remembers waking up to the sound of the front door, feeling like he was still deep in a dream, because who could be creeping inside at this hour? But then he'd listened to his father opening the fridge, pouring a drink, walking softly upstairs, brushing his teeth. Then the mattress had creaked as he crawled into bed.

Years ago, when Chip's father was a more junior guard, he'd worked shifts through the night. His arrival in the predawn hours would sometimes pull Chip from sleep, and he would lie awake and listen to his parents' voices.

On that night back in February of this year, there had been no voices. Just his father padding around the silent cottage.

Now, at last, he knows what his father had been doing that night in the city: playing in some high-stakes poker game with Mr. Thompson. A game run by Jimmy the Hat.

And both men had lost bad.

"Nah," Zipper says, his voice gone cold. "We ain't done here. We're just getting started, you and me."

At this moment, school seems like some faraway place, a pinhole of light in the lens of a camera. His life on the island is even more distant—the life of a solitary kid whose days blur into one. There is only the humming, jittery world of this case, with its layers peeling back before his eyes. Terrible things are being revealed, yes, but he's riding a wave of adrenaline. He can't help it.

A jolt of shame cools him down. Zipper and Mr. Thompson are talking about his own father, who's in deep trouble! Yet here he sits in his disguise, skipping school and playing detective like it's some kind of game.

The faces of his classmates come back to him from that afternoon at the chalkboard, their odd looks etched in his memory. Is there something they all know about him? Something right in front of his eyes that he can't put his finger on that makes everyone keep their distance? Maybe it's precisely *because* he's the kind of person who gets a charge out of mysteries that ought to terrify him. Who feels alive when strange happenings hit too close to home.

Maybe it's actually Benny Thompson who's the normal one here. A kid who's simply worried about his family and tried to get Chip to mind his own business.

"Bon appétit." The waitress drops off his eggs. Steam rises from the plate. Chip had ordered the eggs as part of his cover, but now he figures he might as well eat them. He adds salt and pepper and digs in. The waitress stops at the booth behind his.

"Anything else for you gentlemen?"

"He'll have an egg cream," Zipper says.

"Sure," the waitress says. "On the house."

"You're a doll, Sheri," Zipper says. The waitress moves down the row. "You see what real juice is, Eddie?" Zipper sounds proud of himself.

"Free egg creams?"

"Okay, wise guy. Here's how it is: I got a heater pointed at your kneecap right now, underneath the table. Lean down and peep it if you want. *Real juice* is the hard fact that I could blow a hole in your leg, in the middle of the breakfast rush at the Silver Spoon, get up and walk out the front door while I wipe my mouth with a paper napkin, and nobody'll say *boo*. Not the cooks, not Sheri, not old Barnaby outside the front door."

Chip pauses with his fork in the air. He can feel a dull ache in his back, like there's an invisible line through Mr. Thompson's leg and the red cushion of the booth, pressing into his spine: the path of the bullet from Zipper's heater. He glances over at the bank of windows facing the street. He'd given Maddie a signal to use if there's trouble outside. He hadn't planned on trouble *inside*.

"You got me, Zipper," Mr. Thompson says. "I know I don't rate in this city, not like you. Just take it easy, okay?"

"How easy I take it's up to you," Zipper says. "Here's how it's gonna be from here on out. A simple piece of business. You want the Hat to get a good report from me, you and the pug gotta kick a little dough my way."

"You can't shake us down!" Eddie's voice rises in anger. "We're already in the Alcatraz thing up to our—"

"Shhhh, you want them to hear you down at city hall? Hush now, Eddie. And consider my offer. I'm only gonna make it once."

"Listen," Mr. Thompson says. "Hiram and I are in this mess because we lost at your boss's poker game. We don't have extra scratch kicking around. We're already working off a debt to the Hat. As you well know."

"There's a long list of things that ain't my problem, and that's number one."

"Come on, Zipper. Be fair."

Zipper laughs. It sounds like a strangled bird. "That's rich, Eddie."

"Listen to me." The desperation in Mr. Thompson's voice makes Chip's heart pound. Listening to men he thinks of as strong being scared out of their wits is frightening. He wishes he were anywhere but here. He wishes he'd gone to school. Yet he forces himself to stay put.

"Please," Mr. Thompson says, "I'm already sticking my neck out so far for the Hat. There's nothing left. This'll ruin me."

"So we'll start small," Zipper says. "Same place next Monday, this booth right here. You come with another hundred clams, or the Hat gets an earful about how you're not doing your job." He pauses. "Or maybe I'll just put one in your kneecap for giggles."

Chip feels a light thunk: Mr. Thompson's back, slumping against the seat. "There's no way I can get that kind of money in a week," he says softly.

"I'm sure you and the pug can scrape it together."

The waitress comes to their booth. "Egg cream for the gentleman."

"Thanks, darling," Zipper says. Chip hears him stand up. "I'll leave you to enjoy that, Eddie. Have a nice day."

Chip lowers his eyes to his eggs as Zipper saunters past him and out the front door. Behind him, there is only stillness. Mr. Thompson does not move. Chip imagines he is staring into the foam of his drink.

A hundred dollars! Zipper might as well have asked for the moon.

His father and Mr. Thompson are in big trouble. Chip has to talk to Maddie.

He fishes in his pocket, sets his last two quarters on the table, and heads for the exit.

CHAPTER 14

hip's back with Maddie in the alley across from the Silver Spoon when Mr. Thompson exits. Barnaby, the man in baggy clothes by the front door, rattles his change mug. Mr. Thompson hands him a paper cup with a straw sticking out.

"Egg cream," Chip says. He slides the too-big hat and fake glasses into his backpack.

"He hates egg creams," Maddie says.

"It was on the house."

Barnaby raises the cup in thanks. Mr. Thompson thrusts his hands into his pockets and heads down the hill toward the waterfront. The wind kicks up and he lowers his head. Chip and Maddie watch him disappear.

"It's weird," Maddie says.

A moment passes. She doesn't elaborate. "What is?" Chip asks. He hasn't told her anything yet. It's all too much. Mr. Thompson and his own father, the "pug," are in deep with Jimmy the Hat. Gambling debts they're paying off by working for gangsters.

Zipper's words echo inside his head, that reedy voice on a loop: *This whole Alcatraz scheme. This whole Alcatraz scheme. This whole Alcatraz scheme.*

"Seeing my dad out in the city," Maddie says. "Spying on him. Not being in school on a Monday. And San Francisco just goes on like everything's normal. Sometimes the island feels like the middle of everything, but it's really not, you know?" Maddie leans against the brick wall of the alley. Then she pushes off the wall and paces into the shadows and back toward Chip. Her restlessness infects him. He fights the urge to ditch the alley, run all the way back down to the pier, and wait for the ferry to take him home. He makes himself stay in the moment. After all, Maddie is here and they're in this together now.

"I know what you mean," he says.

When you have a friend, Chip's pretty sure you can't just leave them behind whenever you feel like it. He banishes the thought of hightailing it back to the pier. He feels his face get hot. They're not *friends*, not really, he reminds himself. Last week, she hired him. Today, she followed him. That's all.

"What happened in there, Chip?"

He pulls a toothpick from his pocket and works it back and forth between his fingers, thumb to pinkie, pinkie to thumb.

Then he snaps it in half. He'd practically flown across the street to talk to her and now doesn't know where to begin.

She quits pacing to stare him down. "Spill it."

He scratches the top of his head. The wool hat had been itchy. "I took a plant in the back, right behind your dad and Zipper."

"Zipper?"

"Jimmy the Hat's goon. All skin and bones. Real weasel." Maddie's eyes go wide. Chip decides to leave out the part about the gun underneath the table. "Anyway, I listened in. It turns out your dad and my dad owe Jimmy the Hat money. They're on the hook for a poker game where they lost big."

"Jimmy the Hat comes to your house for poker night?"

Chip blinks. "What? No. Our dads went into the city to play at a high-stakes game he runs."

"Oh." She pauses. "Why would they do that?"

He tosses the broken toothpick into a pile of trash bags huddled against the wall like a sleeping bear. "Why'd they go all the way into the city to play cards with gangsters? I don't know," he says. "But now they're caught up in some kind of Alcatraz scheme as a way to pay back the Hat."

Chip goes on to tell her about Zipper's demand for an extra hundred bucks on top of whatever they owe the Hat. "I think it's called extortion," Chip says, using a word he'd heard on *Hall of Justice* for the first time in his life. A word that brings to mind plots hatched in back rooms. Ticking clocks. The sweat of desperation.

Maddie kicks at a pile of gravel. The buckles on her Mary Janes shine, even in the dim light of the alley. "This Zipper's a piece of work. Where are they gonna get an extra hundred if they already owe the Hat money?"

Chip flashes to Zipper's cold words. *Not my problem.*

"They're caught in the rain all right," Chip says. Suddenly, a slice of light appears in the brick wall just down the alley. The light widens to a rectangle. A big-bellied man in a bloodstained apron tosses out a garbage bag. It hits the ground with a wet smack. The light disappears as the door slams.

"So we go to the cops," Maddie says. "We tell them everything we know. They'll sort things out." She turns and walks to the mouth of the alley. Outside, a group of sailors on leave from the navy rush past, their uniforms a mass of white.

"Hold up," Chip says, hot on her heels. "We can't do that."

She whirls around. He recognizes the look in her eyes from earlier, when she explained why she hired him in the first place. There are things that are true and things we *want* to be true. Like a square and a circle, they can't ever overlap. But the urge to force them together is a powerful one.

"We don't have a choice," she says, her voice pitching higher while her eyes bore into his. She's daring him to stop her. He wonders what a true friend would do. Go along with her plan? Is that the job of a friend, to be steered this way and that, even when you know it's the wrong direction? "Our dads are guards at Alcatraz and these guys are gangsters. When we explain everything, they'll arrest this Zipper guy, and Jimmy the Hat, and—"

"It doesn't work like that."

"Just because you're obsessed with some stupid TV detective, you think you know how it *works*, Chip?"

Her words sting. For a moment his grip on the day falters. The disguise he wore inside the Silver Spoon seems impossibly silly. He's just a kid skipping school to go running around the city playing grown-up. If they slink back to school now, maybe he can come up with some excuse, rejoin his class without much of a fuss. Maddie can go to the cops if she wants; it's none of his business.

She glares back at him while, all around them, San Francisco churns its way through another morning. The city does not care if they go to school. It does not care if their fathers are squeezed dry by the most fearsome gangster on the West Coast, this great unfeeling place that's as monstrous as it is beautiful.

Chip reaches out and puts his hand on Maddie's shoulder like his mother used to do when he was upset. He doesn't squeeze or apply pressure. He just lays it there with the lightest touch. The reassurance of human contact. No more and no less. He doesn't know if this is what a friend would do, or a partner in solving crime, or anything in between. It just feels right. He meets her eyes.

"I don't know how it all works," he says. "But I know what I saw your dad doing with the raincoats." He tells her about the strange raft, about Zipper referring to *the Alcatraz scheme*. "Whatever they're doing, it's not baking for a church potluck. It's something big and hush-hush."

He feels her body sag a little as her resolve ebbs away. "All right," she says. "No cops." He lowers his arm. "So what do we do?" she asks.

He tries to put on a casual smile, as if he's got it all under control.

Maddie closes one eye and studies his expression. "You look like Daffy Duck when he's plotting a dumb caper. The way his mouth—"

"Beak."

"—curls up into his face and his eyelids go down."

Chip kills the grin. "I've got a plan."

She folds her arms across her chest. "What kind of a plan?"

He slings the backpack over his shoulder and steps out into the gray wash of the morning light. His mind hums, the half-formed idea falling into place. "I'll tell you on the way."

Across the street, Barnaby pulls open the door of the Silver Spoon and holds it for a pair of old-lady twins in matching hats. Maddie hesitates, then follows Chip out onto the sidewalk. A parade of motorcycles roars past. "On the way to where?"

Chip's heart pounds. He's once again buoyed by the bright shining possibilities of peeling back the layers, of ripping the mystery apart to find the truth at its core. "Just come on!"

Reluctantly, she falls in beside him. "You're not telling me because it's such a bad plan, you know I won't go along with it."

"Wrong." They cut through a line of customers snaking back from a coffee cart. The smell of freshly baked pastries comes and goes. "It's a good plan." He feels the heat of her glare. "A *great* plan."

CHAPTER

This is a terrible plan!"

The corner of Columbus and Pacific is a bustling hive of activity, but Maddie's voice hits him loud and clear.

It's what Jake Hall would do, he stops himself from saying out loud. Somehow, he doesn't think Maddie will find it convincing.

"This is our only shot to help our dads," he says.

He's led her off Telegraph Hill and down into North Beach, where Little Italy meets Chinatown. Sedans trail streetcars crawling down the wide avenue, and the mingling scents of restaurants gearing up for the lunch crowd are dizzying: lasagna and lo mein, eggplant and egg rolls.

Just ahead is the sign for the Andromeda Café, big block letters surrounded by unlit marquee bulbs. Chip's only ever seen it in grainy black and white in the *San Francisco Chronicle*.

"Looks like it's closed," Maddie says. "How do you know he's going to be here?"

"Don't you read the papers?"

"Yeah, the funnies."

"This is his joint. It's where people go to do business with him."

"Business." She shakes her head and glances up at the café sign. "Maybe Benny was right," she mutters. "Maybe it's better not to know."

"Benny's dead wrong."

Chip feels like he's fully inhabiting his skin, becoming the person he was born to be. In this moment, he knows exactly what to do and what to say. "When we get in there, remember—"

The front door of the café swings open. A man and a woman burst out, laughing. He's a big lunk in a dark suit, clutching an envelope. She's in a green dress with a matching jacket and big pearl earrings. The woman lights up a cigar and tosses away the match while the man eyes Chip and Maddie with mild contempt.

"Kids today," he says to the woman. She blows smoke. The man steps toward them. "When I was your age, I had the good sense not to roam the streets when I ditched school. You ever heard of truant officers?"

"Aww," the woman says, "leave 'em alone, Freddie."

The man shrugs his massive shoulders. He tucks the envelope into his pocket. "You bambini wanna get pinched, that's your business. But don't say I didn't warn you."

Chip hesitates. He was hoping for more time to talk over the plan with Maddie. But now these two are lingering outside the café. And they don't look like they're going anywhere.

To his surprise, Maddie beats him to the punch.

"We're here to talk to Jimmy the Hat," she tells Freddie. The woman bursts out laughing, which turns to coughing. She doubles over, wreathed in smoke, holding her belly.

Freddie doesn't laugh. He doesn't even smirk. His eyes slide from Maddie to Chip and back again. Chip picks out the bulge of a pistol holstered in a shoulder rig beneath his jacket, like a cop. *Maybe*, he thinks, *this guy* is *a cop*. It's no secret that Jimmy the Hat has police officers, judges, and politicians in his pocket. Freddie's gaze lingers on Chip: small, unblinking eyes, taking his measure.

"He's gonna want to hear this," Chip says. He tries to sound sure of himself, but his words are laced with fear. Some distant part of him wonders why he hasn't been afraid—*really afraid*— until this moment. Now the sense that he's an impostor, a little kid in a costume, makes him feel small. Freddie's eyes narrow. Chip thinks he should have snuck out of the Silver Spoon the minute Zipper pulled his heater. He should have scooped Maddie from the alley and hightailed it back to the pier. He should have—

"The Hat's a busy man," Freddie says. "Give me the skinny and I'll pass it along."

Chip wants to wriggle out of Freddie's hard gaze. Paranoia swells: Does Freddie know his father? Does he recognize Chip, somehow? Was he at the poker game with Zipper, watching Hiram Carter and Eddie Thompson blow their money?

"It's personal," Maddie says. She sounds more confident

than Chip. Gratitude washes over him. He's glad he's not alone on this job.

"It's about the old neighborhood," Chip adds. He has no idea where Jimmy the Hat grew up, but on TV the mobsters are always doing favors for people from the "old neighborhood."

"C'mon, Freddie," the woman says, pulling a spotless white cloth from a sequined purse and dabbing her eyes. "Quit hassling the kids."

"Can it," he says without looking at her.

She makes a throaty noise of annoyance and tosses the smoldering cigar into the street. A bread truck runs it over. Without another word, she walks away.

"Lemme see your bag," Freddie says. Chip hands over his backpack. The man's big mitts rifle through it, then he tosses it back.

"Arms up," he says. Chip raises his arms. The man gives him a quick, expert pat-down. Then he turns to Maddie and they go through the same routine. Satisfied that they aren't armed or wired up, Freddie stands aside.

"Back room," he says. Chip and Maddie duck into the dim interior. The place isn't open yet, and the legs from upside-down chairs poke up like thin stalagmites. "One more thing."

Chip turns. Freddie's bulk fills the doorway. Gray light squeezes around him in soft shapes. "I wouldn't put it past Hoover to send a couple of kids." Chip knows Freddie means Hoover as in *J. Edgar Hoover*, FBI director. "If I find out you're snitches, I'll kill you."

He slams the door.

CHAPTER

Chip moves through the gloom of the café, Maddie at his side. The smell of stale sweat and spilled drinks washes over him. His shoes squelch on the sticky floor. Wan light drifts in through closed blinds. He catches their reflections in the long mirror behind the bar, lost in a murky haze.

The whole place screams *You don't belong here*. It stinks of late-night skulking, hushed conversations in corner booths, the metallic click of switchblades in the dark. He wonders if a kid's ever set foot inside before now.

Freddie's words echo: *I'll kill you.*

Maddie's right—this is a terrible plan. Without thinking about it, he takes her hand. He's not sure if it's an apology or something else. She squeezes. He squeezes back. It fortifies him with a jolt of warmth. Despite his fear, his mind flashes to the note his father left him with Friday's fish dinner. He wonders if Maddie would want to go to a baseball game with him this summer. Surely, it would be a normal thing for one friend to ask another. Just two more pals among the thousands of kids at Candlestick Park to cheer on the San Francisco Giants, his father beaming in the seat next to them, waving a hand for the popcorn man . . .

Warmth turns to heat that rises up his neck. *Grow up, Chip. She's worried about her dad, is all. Bigger fish to fry.* He pulls his hand away, banishes the thought of a baseball game. Together they stand before a door marked PRIVATE.

"Can I help you?" a voice calls from the shadows.

Chip jumps. A figure slinks out of a dark hallway that leads to the kitchen: a woman in a sharp tan suit, all buttons and big lapels, holding a leather briefcase.

"Freddie sent us in," Chip says.

"We're here to see Jimmy the Hat," Maddie says.

The woman's mouth flicks into a quick smile. "He hates that name, you know. He doesn't even really like hats all that much. I mean, he wears one, but so what? Everybody wears a hat. Might as well be called Jimmy the Shirt. Word to the wise, you want to get on his good side, stick with 'Mr. Lanza.'"

Her brown hair flips up in the back like Jackie's, the president's wife. She strides over to the bar, lays the briefcase down, and pops the locks. Chip strains to see what's inside. Maddie elbows him.

"Is it okay if we go in?" she asks.

"I'm not Mr. Lanza's secretary," the woman says without

turning around. She begins sifting through papers. "I don't care what you do."

Chip wonders if there's a pistol holstered beneath her jacket, too. Maddie reaches out and turns the doorknob. It's unlocked. She pushes it open. Chip expects to step into a sumptuous lair, with rich mahogany furniture and red velvet walls, some pricey foreign cat prowling the rug, mewling for its fancy food.

What he finds is the back room of a café. Linoleum floors, metal shelves full of wine cases and cleaning supplies, a dingy window that looks out at the brick walls of the alley. Folding chairs ring a pair of card tables. Between them sits an old man at a desk that looks like it was scavenged from a yard sale. He's doused in yellow light from a lamp that hangs from the ceiling by a silver chain. The brim of his fedora casts a shadow down his face, and his eyes peer out from behind thick glasses. Bottles of all shapes and sizes crowd the desk. He tilts one of the bottles to fill a spoon with thick, buttery liquid.

"Here," Jimmy the Hat says, carefully extending the spoon across the desk. He lifts his head to regard his visitors. "Try this."

Chip glances at Maddie. He's not sure what he was expecting, but it certainly wasn't this. The liquid in the spoon catches the light. It's viscous and slippery, like cough medicine. He tries to get a handle on the situation.

"Go ahead," the Hat urges. His tone is almost gentle, a school-teacher trying to entice a student to pick up a book. Chip tries to read the situation. It would be ridiculous to poison his visitors before he heard what they had to say—wouldn't it?

He figures he ought to get on the Hat's good side. He goes

over to the desk, pops the spoon in his mouth, and swallows.

"Olive oil," he says, puzzled.

"Yeah, yeah," the Hat says, impatient, like it was obvious from the get-go. "But what's wrong with it?"

Chip shrugs. "Tastes good to me."

The Hat's palm comes down hard on the table, startling Chip. The bottles jump.

"There's a bum note in there somewhere," the Hat says, putting the spoon down on a napkin. "Like a violin out of tune."

He dips a finger into the bottle and touches it to the tip of his tongue. Lost in thought, he sits quietly for a moment. Then he sighs. "My father, God rest his soul, made olive oil when he came to this country. Just a small grove at first, the best you ever tasted. People used to drink it like wine, wash their hair in it. And I'll tell you something else, it *stayed* good. You could stick a bottle of Lanza Olive Oil in your cellar, keep it more or less cool, and ten years later you break it out for a salad, it's still fresh as the day it was made. That's the cold pressing. Then what do you suppose happened?"

"Um," Maddie says.

"Nazis!" He points a finger at them. "Hitler invades Poland and our boys go over to sort him out, and all of a sudden this country's got shortages. War rations and whatnot. Olive oil floods the black market. We can't make it fast enough. My father, God rest his soul, died in 1937 and the quality control died with him. I've spent twenty years trying to get this back to the original recipe. The olive oil we had before the war. But there's *always*." He strikes the table again. *"Something. Wrong."*

"I'm sorry," Chip says.

Jimmy the Hat folds his arms on the table and stares at Chip. "What are the ingredients in olive oil?"

"Olives?" Chip guesses.

"Hey, Angie!" Jimmy the Hat yells at the door.

"What?" the woman out in the café yells back.

"We got ourselves a real connoisseur here!"

"That's nice, Mr. Lanza!"

He lowers his gaze to Chip. His eyes are magnified behind his glasses. "What else?"

Chip racks his brain.

"Water?" Maddie says.

"Correct. Olives and water." He opens a different bottle and takes a big sniff. His mouth wrinkles in a vacant, ecstatic smile. "The old stuff. One hundred percent pure." He replaces the cap, then gestures to the first bottle with disdain. "I ask my guys down at the plant, I say, *What are you putting in this garbage?* Olives and water, boss, they tell me. Same as your father, God rest his soul." He shakes his head. "But I know there's some filthy *additive*." His face pinches. "Some *chemical* that's found its way into the production line."

Jimmy the Hat is looking at them expectantly, like he's waiting for a fresh perspective on his olive oil problem. Chip figures he should say something.

"Maybe you could have it tested in a lab?"

Jimmy the Hat's lips hint at a smile. "A real idea man. Truly your father's son."

Chip tries to keep his mouth from dropping open, betraying

his surprise. He's been caught off guard since he stepped into this room.

The aging mobster holds out an open palm, indicating a pair of folding chairs facing the desk. "Sit."

It doesn't sound like a request. Chip and Maddie sit. The folding chairs squeak.

"I saw Hiram Carter box. Fifty-three, I think it was." He nods at Chip. "You would've been in short pants."

"Did he win?"

Jimmy the Hat laughs. It's an odd sound, like a machine gun of *he-he-he-he*. "He could've taken the guy's head clean off with that right hook of his. But no. Ate canvas in the fourth round."

"Oh." Chip is too young to remember his father's boxing career. He's never thought about his father being knocked out cold before. Falling like a sack of potatoes to the mat.

"About as good a boxer as he is a card player, your pop." Jimmy the Hat shakes his head, like it's especially tragic. "Anyway. This a social call, or what?"

The mobster's too-big eyes regard Chip from behind thick lenses. He feels like he's under a microscope. Freddie's words echo once again: *I'll kill you.* He needs to change the energy. Reset the table. He sticks a toothpick in his mouth, tastes pine. He tries to think of how to begin.

"We've got something you'll want to hear, Mr. Lanza," Maddie says, saving him once again. And once again, Chip's grateful he's not alone.

Jimmy the Hat folds his hands and sits back in his chair. "And your pop's the other Alcatraz bull, I take it."

Maddie averts her eyes. This is harder than Chip thought, sitting here with this man who could have them tossed in the bay with cement shoes at the snap of his fingers. This man who knows exactly who their fathers are. A faint smell of bleach hangs in the room. Chip shifts in his seat. The chair squeaks.

"Don't worry," Jimmy the Hat says. "I got all day. You want a sandwich?"

"I just had eggs," Chip says.

"Spill it, kid." The mobster's voice gets cold and steely.

Chip takes a deep breath and begins. "Your, um . . ." He doesn't know what to call Zipper, exactly. *Goon* doesn't seem like something he should say to the boss of San Francisco's most powerful family.

"Helper guy," Maddie suggests.

"Employee," Chip says.

"Associate," Maddie says.

"Zipper," Chip says. Jimmy the Hat looks mildly interested.

"He's running his own game, right under your nose," Chip says, the words spilling out easily now. "He's squeezing our dads for extra cash." Chip tells the man what he overheard in the Silver Spoon: Zipper's extortion plot. According to the mob bosses on *Hall of Justice*, they don't take kindly to their underlings operating scams without giving them a cut. This whole plan hinges on Jimmy the Hat feeling betrayed by Zipper, and in turn feeling grateful to Chip and Maddie for bringing him the truth.

"And there's no way our dads can get extra cash to pay off Zipper, too," Maddie finishes up, "since they already owe *you* so much money."

"So Zipper's really just making things harder for you, working his own scheme behind your back," Chip adds.

Jimmy the Hat pulls a cork from a bottle of olive oil. He holds it up to the light, turning it slowly in his fingers, lost in thought. Then he pops it back in the bottle and refolds his hands on the desk. He looks from Maddie to Chip.

"I take it you're not bringing me this information out of the kindness of your little hearts."

"Whatever you're doing with Alcatraz," Maddie says, "leave our dads out of it. Please."

"Mr. Lanza," Chip adds. "Sir."

"The bum note," the mob boss says after a moment. "The chemical messing with the process." He uncorks another bottle, dips a finger, tastes it, makes a face. "Is this filthy chemical named Zipper?" He recorks the bottle and leans forward. "Or is it *you*?"

Chip bites down hard on the toothpick. A cold knot twists up his guts. This is a terrible plan. He's a fool to think he could bargain with San Francisco's public enemy number one, a man who had worked the system and evaded arrest for decades.

"No," Maddie protests. "We're telling you the truth."

Jimmy the Hat smiles, but he doesn't look amused. "We'll see about that." His eyes go to the door to the back room. "Angie!" he calls out.

"Mr. Lanza!" she calls back.

"Get Freddie in here!"

CHAPTER

Big man, small room. Freddie lurks with his arms folded, sleeves of his jacket riding up his meaty forearms. He leans back against the door, blocking their exit. His presence is like a sudden appliance, a fridge that just popped in, humming with bad vibes.

Freddie stares Chip and Maddie down while they relate their tale about Zipper's rogue play. His face betrays nothing. When they finish, he looks to his boss and waits for an order.

"Bring Zipper to me," the Hat says. "We need to have a little chat."

Freddie hesitates. "Everybody skims," he says carefully. "Zipper's no different. It's just a hundred clams we're talking about here, boss." Chip is surprised: On TV, goons never voice an opinion to the boss. He feels extra vulnerable: Freddie would rather defend a weasel like Zipper than give Chip and Maddie the benefit of the doubt.

"Rackets are one thing," the Hat tells his underling. "My capos take a taste of the sports book, the numbers, a couple of TVs fell off the back of a truck, that's a time-honored tradition. They know I know. And I know they know that I know. But Alcatraz is a whole other bottle of olive oil. We only get one shot at this. That little donnola messes this up . . ."

Freddie hesitates. He stink-eyes Chip and Maddie, looking like he just drank spoiled milk. Then he opens his mouth.

"I gotta say, boss, I mean no disrespect, but this Alcatraz thing . . . it's gonna bring down a lotta heat if it goes sideways."

"Angie!" Jimmy the Hat calls out.

"Mr. Lanza!" she calls back through the door.

"I pay Freddie here for his opinions?"

"Nope!"

When Freddie doesn't move right away, Jimmy the Hat slams a palm down on the table. The bottles jump. Chip reaches for Maddie's hand. He feels like he's spiraling into a bad dream full of nonsense corridors and to claw his way out will be nearly impossible.

"*San Francisco is my ship!*" the mob boss screams. "*And Alcatraz is a festering barnacle on its hull!*"

"I gotcha, boss," Freddie says. He beats a retreat. The door closes behind him. Jimmy the Hat takes a deep breath and shuts his eyes. Despite his fear, Chip glances at Maddie. The pieces are so close to falling into place: the raft made of raincoats, all this talk of *the Alcatraz scheme*, Jimmy the Hat forcing their dads—a pair of Alcatraz guards—to work on some secret plot.

Coming here might have been a terrible plan, but if they'd just slunk back to school after the Silver Spoon, they wouldn't be this close to the source of the scheme, to finding out what it is, exactly.

And after the *what* comes the *how* and the *why*.

Chip knows he should keep his mouth shut. They're in no position to do anything but hope to get out of here alive. He looks at Maddie again. He can't read her face. He wishes he could freeze time for a minute, just so they can talk things out. If they were real friends, maybe they could communicate without words and he would know what she wanted to do. But that kind of relationship takes time, he figures.

Jimmy the Hat's eyes open. His gentle demeanor returns. "A barnacle," he repeats, his voice calm. "A *lesion* on my city. And what do we do to lesions?"

Chip frowns. He doesn't know what a *lesion* is. He glances at Maddie. She shrugs.

"We cut them off," the mob boss says. He mimes an invisible slice with a scalpel. Then he stares off between Chip and Maddie at something only he can see. A look of great satisfaction lights up his face, like a sunbeam flashing through a dark room.

Maddie mouths *Let's go* at Chip. Her eyes flick toward the door. With Freddie gone, they'd only have to make it past Angie out in the café, and Chip figures it's fifty-fifty whether she's inclined to give chase.

But if they leave now, they'll still be in the dark.

Jake Hall would keep pushing till he got what he wanted.

"You're going to cut Alcatraz off?" Chip says, prodding.

Instantly, the mob boss snaps out of his reverie. His magnified eyes narrow behind his lenses. "I gotta hand it to you, I thought you knew the whole long and the short of it. Walking in here like you did with that whole rap about Zipper, looking to cut a deal for your padri. But you're just a couple of kids stumbling around in the dark."

Life on the island seems impossibly far away. Chip feels unmoored from reality, adrift on a perilous voyage. For a split second he wishes he *was* wearing a wire, working for J. Edgar Hoover and the FBI. At least then, there would be grown-ups listening, armed agents on the other end ready to rush in and save him from himself.

"Can't you just leave our dads alone?" Maddie is pleading now.

"No," the Hat says. "They're in too deep. But I'm going to give you two choices. Number one: You can get up and walk outta here right now. Nobody's gonna stop you."

Maddie stands up and heads for the door.

"What's number two?" Chip asks.

"Chip," Maddie says, pausing with her hand on the doorknob. "Who cares. Come on."

"Number two," Jimmy the Hat says, "you can stick around and I'll give you the straight dope on the whole Alcatraz scheme. Everything your fathers are involved in and more. I'll lay it all out for you real nice."

"Why would you do that?"

"Maybe it's a gesture of goodwill and appreciation. Or

maybe it isn't. You leave now, you'll never know."

Chip looks at Maddie. She shakes her head. "You go," he tells her. "I'm gonna stay."

Maddie looks like she's already halfway out the door in a puff of cartoon smoke, the girl who remains a fading mirage. She takes a deep breath and lets go of the doorknob.

"Okay," she says. Slowly, like she's forcing one foot in front of the other, she crosses the small room and sits down. The chair creaks.

Chip looks at her. He has so many questions. Is she doing this for him? Because she's worried about him? Like someone might be worried about a friend? He doesn't believe that could possibly be true. He can count the number of hours they've been hanging out on one hand. Is that enough time to consider someone a friend?

His mind reels. He wonders what he would have done if the situation had been reversed and it had been *his* hand on the doorknob. He tries to communicate with a glance. He wishes he could tell her how they can't help their fathers if they remain in the dark. How the truth is always the goal, no matter what.

Jimmy the Hat watches from behind his thick glasses. "Number two it is," he says. Chip swears he detects the hint of a smile. That dreamy satisfaction returns. He clears his throat.

"I'm going to wipe Alcatraz off the map," he announces. Then he sits back and waits for them to take this in.

Chip imagines air strikes, bombs, panic. Apocalyptic visions of the island sinking into the bay. Jimmy the Hat reads his face.

"The Rock's gonna destroy itself from within, kid. Nice and

poetic like." He holds up a hand and forms his words like he's reading a headline. "Inmates Escape from Escape-Proof Prison."

Of course. It all makes sense. The raincoat raft. The hush-hush scheme. The reason the mob boss needs two Alcatraz guards to do his dirty work from the inside.

"You're planning a prison break," Maddie says.

Jimmy the Hat sits back in his chair. "And you two are going to help me."

CHAPTER

I don't get it."

Chip's father dabs at the corners of his mouth with a cloth napkin that Chip's mother had embroidered with sparrows. The dainty motion is at odds with his massive hands and their scarred knuckles. "Skipping school isn't like you, Chipper."

His father doesn't sound angry. Just confused. Maybe suspicious, too. But Chip feels suspicion everywhere now. It hangs in the air like a bad smell. Meat gone rancid, a rodent dead in the walls.

Chip picks up his fork and moves his green beans around his plate.

"Look at me," his father says. Chip raises his eyes to his

father's bent nose, bashed out of joint long ago. He wonders if it happened during the fight Jimmy the Hat attended. The one where his father ate canvas in the fourth round. There are bags under his father's eyes. Thickness is slowly taking over his body, cushioning the hard bands of muscle that still cord through his arms and shoulders. "Do you have anything to say for yourself?"

Chip is too weary to even come up with a decent fib. His brain feels like mush. He needs a root beer float. "I just didn't feel like going today."

Chip's father takes a sip of his milk. He regards his son in silence. Next door, the Harrison kids are making a ruckus in the yard. Somebody says *You're it!*

Chip braces himself. The school eventually reached his father on the phone in the guardroom at work. His father had received the unwelcome news that Chip hadn't shown up at school today, for the first time ever. Naturally, Hiram Carter sprang into action, assuming the worst. An accident, a kidnapping. Police had been mobilized; all-points bulletins crackled across the wires.

Then, an hour before the final bell, Chip and Maddie straggled into school with no excuse for their absence.

If his father found it extra suspicious that Chip had played hooky with the daughter of his partner in crime, he hasn't said anything. Chip watches as his father mops up gravy with a slightly burned biscuit. He wonders what his father would do if he knew the truth: that his son has just been to see Jimmy the Hat himself.

But he and Maddie promised each other they would not blab like a couple of stool pigeons. Not to their parents, not to the cops. Not until they figure out their next move.

So the secrets between Chip and his dad pile up like poker chips.

Chip quits arranging his green beans, picks up his own biscuit, and breaks it into crumbly pieces. He figures he'll endure a lecture, then do the dishes while his father trudges upstairs to knock the heavy bag around.

"It's my fault," his father says.

Chip's hands go still. He gazes into the depths of his milk. His mind struggles to connect these words to the anger he'd expected from his father. "Dad" is all he can manage to sputter out.

"I haven't been there for you lately," his father continues. He grips the embroidered napkin tight, balls it up in his fist. In an echo of Jimmy the Hat, he gazes off into some hidden middle distance. "I look in the mirror, you know what I see?"

Chip shakes his head.

"Me neither," his father says softly. "You know I came from nothing. My own pop, your grandad, he wasn't"—his father searches for the word—"*kind*. Or, I don't know what he was. Times were different. It wasn't all his fault, he just had his ways, is all." Despite the fresh anxieties sprung on him by the day's events, Chip is enthralled. He's never met his grandparents on his dad's side. He's not sure when they died, exactly, but he knows they're not around. And his father's a closed book when it comes to the past. His father's eyes linger on the embroidered sparrow. His finger traces the curve of its tucked wing.

"Boxing was—boxing made me *something*, for a little while." He begins idly smoothing out the napkin. "But it wasn't until your mother came along that I really became *somebody*." He smiles, taps the napkin. "She was bird-watching in the park. I guess you know that story."

Chip's heard this one a million times. His father, a few years out of the army, trying to make a real go of the amateur fighting skills he'd honed overseas. Up on a grassy hill by the Great Highway, hitting his trainer's punch mitts, sweating buckets. His mother, stalking a great blue heron with a pair of binoculars. Absentminded, popping out of the underbrush as the heron took flight, wandering right between his father and the trainer. Startled, both of them. Their eyes meeting, his father suddenly forgetting about his right hook. His mother forgetting about the heron.

"I've been searching for something since she . . ." His father trails off. Chip wishes his father would just say *died*, but he never does. The absence of the unspoken word is more horrible than the sound of it spoken aloud. There's dishonesty in the silence— but then again, there's dishonesty crowding in on them both from all directions now.

"I guess I've just been a little lost without her," his father says.

Lost. Chip turns the word over in his mind. So lost that he wandered into a card game with a bunch of gangsters? So lost that he got in too deep with Jimmy the Hat?

"I guess I have, too," Chip says. Both of them lost. So lost that they're going to help prisoners escape from the supposedly escape-proof federal penitentiary that looms above their house.

"How are you, though, Chip?" his father asks after a moment. "How are you *really*?"

Chip is caught off guard. Silently, he tries out a few quips, snappy lines cribbed from Jake Hall. None of them feel right. He drops the armor—not all the way, but enough, for now, to toss out a real answer.

"I'm okay," he says. "Yeah. Pretty good."

It's not exactly a torrent of honesty, but it'll have to do.

His father looks him in the eyes. Chip senses fear there, maybe something like shame. "I noticed, lately," his father begins deliberately. He reaches for the napkin, then stops himself and holds his big hands in his lap. "That you haven't been hanging out with the other kids, so much."

Chip feels like shrinking down into a puddle on his seat, dripping to the floor, pooling in a crack in the floorboards, out of sight. His father waits a moment. When Chip doesn't say anything, he continues.

"I get it, you know. Sometimes, it's easier just to be alone."

Chip flashes to the unreadable looks his classmates gave him that day at school when he turned away from the chalkboard. "I went bowling," he protests. "I bowled with people."

And just today, he doesn't dare say out loud, *Maddie and I had quite a time in the big city.*

His father's face doesn't change. "Right," he says. "I know you did. I'm just trying to say—"

"I'm fine, Dad."

"Just listen to me." His father closes his eyes, takes a deep breath, opens them. "What I'm trying to say is, it's okay to be alone, if that's what you really want. But that's different from being *lonely*. That's a place I can't let you get to. I won't." He pauses. "You know, I see kids playing ball on the parade ground, every day."

Chip withers under his father's scrutiny. He knows he has to say something. "I don't think they want me to play with them."

"Of course they do!" His father forces a smile. "Anybody with any sense can see you're a great kid."

Chip flashes to the night he walked to the social hall, when he ran into the high school kids leaving Building 64. Susie Porter had politely invited him to walk with their group, until the other boy put a stop to that notion. "They think I'm weird."

"That's a load of bull." His father stands up and carries his empty plate to the sink. It clatters against the dirty dishes. He squirts bright blue dish soap down into the mess with such force that bubbles slip out of the plastic nozzle and float gently upward. Chip watches them pop against the ceiling. Then he watches his father's broad back make jumpy movements as he attacks the dirty dishes with an old sponge.

Chip gets up and scrapes his green beans into the trash, then adds his plate to the pile in the sink. He turns to head upstairs when his father suddenly quits scrubbing.

"I love you, Chipper."

Chip turns back. Suds drip from his father's hands. Chip doesn't know what to say. He hadn't realized it until this moment, but it's been a long time since his father has said this out loud.

He realizes now how much you can miss something you never even realized you lost.

"I love you, too, Dad."

"I'm going to get us off this rock," his father says with grim determination. As if they had been marooned here for a few days instead of a lifetime. As if living on Alcatraz Island isn't all Chip knows. His father wipes his hands on a checkered towel hanging from a handle. "Things are going to change. I promise."

Chip fights the urge to let this lie. Without tipping his hand about what he knows, he pushes—gently. "What about your job?"

His father goes back to scrubbing, this time with vigorous energy, as if the mere thought of change has jolted him with new life. "There are other jobs. Other places. You want to live in a big city. I know you do."

"Like San Francisco?"

"Maybe even bigger! Why not Chicago? Or New York? Heck, why not *London*?"

"What about Alcatraz?"

There's a little hitch in his father's movement, a quick pause before he resumes scrubbing. "Alcatraz won't be around forever."

Chip can't help himself. "What do you mean?"

His father sets the last plate in the drying rack. He looks out the window above the sink. Night is falling fast now, dusk tipping into darkness. Limbs of the spindly tree out front carve slate-colored shapes out of the sky. A feeling of deep foreboding gathers at the base of Chip's spine.

"Everything ends," his father says. "But you and me—we'll keep on keeping on. Together, forever. I promise."

"Then let's go *now*," Chip says, the words tumbling out faster than he can think. It's not a plan he came up with. It's nothing but pure impulse. "Let's just get out of here, tomorrow morning, on the very first boat. We can go straight to the train station and get out of California, even."

It's a better idea than anything he and Maddie can cook up. Whether they fall deeper into Jimmy the Hat's clutches or figure out how to defy him, odds that they all survive this are slim. But what if they simply opt out completely?

His father looks pained. "I can't run away."

But Chip's off to the races. He barely hears his father. "We can get sandwiches on the way. And pack some clothes, whatever we can carry. We don't need much. And—"

"Chip."

"I've got a few bucks saved up—"

"Chip!"

He falls silent. His father turns back to the window, stares out into the deepening night. "I have to see something through first. I can't just up and leave."

"Okay," Chip says. He can see his father's reflection, just beginning to ghost the window glass. He watches his father's face change shape as thoughts run through his head. He looks like he's locked in a struggle.

"If something's going on with you," his father says, "you can always talk to me about it."

"I will," Chip says. *Same goes for you*, he thinks.

Neither of them says a word.

The moment of silence stretches onward. The reflection of his father's face composes itself. He turns his head to shoot Chip a sad little smile. "No more skipping school. Promise me."

"I promise."

His dad lifts a plate from the drying rack and begins rubbing it with a hand towel until it squeaks. Chip stands at the threshold of the kitchen, watching his father's mouth form words he can't hear as he makes tight little circles around the plate.

"I told your mother we'd get a dishwasher one of these days," he says.

"I remember."

"We never did."

Chip turns and heads up to his room.

*T*HWACK.

Down the hall, his father deals the heavy bag a crushing blow. Chip sits cross-legged on his bed, bending over his notebook. His thoughts unspool down the page. Everything he knows about the Alcatraz scheme, neat and organized to sort out the mess in his head.

His father and Eddie Thompson lose big in a card game. They owe Jimmy the Hat.

At the same time, the mob boss is plotting to wipe Alcatraz off the map—this "barnacle" on the underbelly of his city.

The Hat sees a once-in-a-lifetime opportunity in two Alcatraz guards who owe him money. He forces them to aid in his scheme. Hiram Carter and Eddie Thompson start working out ways to help prisoners get away in a big flashy escape—but it all has to look like it's coming from the inside. Hence, the raft made of raincoats.

THWACK.

It sounds like his father is trying to send the heavy bag flying off its chain. Chip glances at the back of his bedroom door, where the light from his bedside lamp just barely hits the framed poster of *True Detective* magazine. On the cover, a man in a trenchcoat and fedora lurks beneath a lonely streetlight. Chip turns back to his notebook.

Thanks to Zipper's attempt to pocket some cash behind his boss's back, Jimmy the Hat finds himself suddenly confronted by the kids of the two Alcatraz guards in his pocket.

This is where the whole thing takes a turn. Chip puts down his pencil. He rubs his eyes and fights the urge to lie down. Sleep is an escape, and he can't let himself escape until he gets this all straight.

He still doesn't know if it was a huge, boneheaded mistake, following Mr. Thompson to the diner, eavesdropping, taking what he found out straight to Jimmy the Hat. His plan to trade the information about Zipper for their fathers' freedom hadn't worked, not even a little bit. It had only pulled them all in further.

He quits scribbling, sets the pencil down, closes his eyes.

THWACK.

He knows he has to face up to what happened today after he made his choice to stay and listen to Jimmy the Hat lay it all out. The devil's bargain he'd walked straight into, dragging Maddie along with him. *Sleep*, he tells himself. But it will still be there in the morning, all of it. Better to face it down now, try to uncover a fresh angle.

He stares out into his room at the clutter atop his dresser—baseball cards, two half-full piggy banks, and a mug that looks like a Campbell's Soup can. He thinks of Zipper's insistence that Mr. Thompson try the egg cream, which ended up in a paper cup in old Barnaby's hands, which Maddie saw from across the street.

Layers upon layers.

His mother died, his father came apart. He started playing high-stakes poker with gangsters, and now here they are.

Chains of cause and effect—the braided threads of any good mystery.

The question is, what's a thread he can pull to make the whole thing unravel without getting them all killed?

THWACK. The whole cottage shakes.

He gets out of bed, paces to his desk, then over to his dresser, where he sifts through a pile of stray coins. He goes to the door and studies the figure on the *True Detective* cover. The man's face is hidden in shadow, hat pulled low, hands thrust deep in his pockets. Could be an overworked office clerk getting some air or a shady goon up to no good. No one knows what's going on in anyone else's head. All you have to judge people by is what they do. If someone were to look at Chip and his father from the outside, would they see a pair of criminals, helping dangerous men escape from the world's most notorious prison? Or would they see two people trying their best who got caught up in something beyond their control?

Every episode of *Hall of Justice*, the cops and the district attorney think Jake Hall is a nuisance, a meddler, even a criminal himself. It's only at the end, when he gets results, that they're forced to admit that maybe he was working for the side of good all along.

But for Chip, right now, that happy ending is hidden by all that must come before it. He goes back to his bed. There's no getting around it now. Jimmy the Hat's words come flooding back, and the reality of what he's been asked to do hits him hard.

He closes his eyes, sees Jimmy the Hat's cold lizard-grin.

. . . And you two are going to help me. You know that fine old mansion up by the lighthouse, where Warden Blackwell lives? A house he don't deserve, not even a little bit? You're going to burn it to the ground.

Chip and Maddie had given him goggle eyes, speechless and horrified.

You'll get a message at school, the mob boss had continued. *That'll be the night you do the job. I stand on the pier and look out across the bay and I don't see a fire, I turn your fathers over to the cops. Instead of getting out of this with their debt to me repaid and nobody else the wiser, they get fifteen to twenty years in a federal lockup. And maybe I'll send Freddie to pay you a visit, too. He's a real people person; you can imagine how much he likes to socialize. We clear?*

All Chip and Maddie could do was nod.

Now, in his bedroom, he opens his eyes. He wishes he could creep down the hall, pick up the phone, and call Maddie, but it's late, and he doesn't know what he'll say if Mr. Thompson answers.

His father's footsteps move down the hall. The water runs in the bathroom sink. He pictures his father splashing his sweaty face.

Then he pictures his father doing time in a federal prison, all because his stupid son thought he could save the day.

Chip kneels on his bed and turns to part the curtains on the small window above his headboard. Outside, the dark expanse of the parade ground yawns like a great void, attached to the bigger emptiness of the dark bay and the vast ocean beyond. Upon the topmost rocky tier of the island, the lighthouse is a grim spire topped with a radiant sunburst that flashes on and off. Beside the lighthouse, a single window glows in the warden's spacious, elegant house. Chip considers what it would take to burn it down. A can of gasoline wouldn't be hard to get—there's a maintenance shed out behind Building 64. Same for matches, those are everywhere. Then he'd just have to find a way into the house, splash the fuel along the carpets and down the drapes, run a thin little stream out the way he came in, set it alight . . .

He shakes his head. He can't believe he's actually picturing it as if it's something he's really going to do. It seems unreal, like taking a flying leap off the lighthouse and soaring into the air above the bay. But he has to do it. Or else.

He turns his attention to the penitentiary itself, the gloomy silhouette he can barely see beyond the lighthouse. The long block of a building, its stark angles cutting slices into the night sky. Somewhere in that maze of cold steel bars and drab corridors, prisoners are preparing for their grand escape . . .

INSIDE

The Watcher is no artist. Other inmates pass the time by sketching or painting. He is always surprised at the skill of some of his fellow prisoners. But he should not be. For men doing life, there is nothing but time.

The Watcher thinks of himself as more of a craftsman. Someone who, with a different path in life, might have made a good engineer. Perhaps even a watchmaker. What he lacks in natural ability, he makes up for in obsessive attention to detail. And patience, of course. The one thing most people lack—even in here.

He lies back on his cot, head propped on a pillow, pretending to read an issue of *Popular Science*. Next to him on the floor is a small stack of magazines available in the prison library. *National Geographic, Esquire, Life.* Some of the men in here avoid magazines like the plague. They do not like to be bombarded with full-color images of life on the outside. Ty Cobb in his Dodgers uniform, Soviet cosmonauts, the movie star Elizabeth Taylor in a Cleopatra costume. But the Watcher is not bothered by it.

Besides, it cannot hurt to be current on the events of the world he will be rejoining very soon.

He turns the page. There is an advertisement for 7UP, a soda he does not particularly care for. A group of youngsters crowd onto a hayride, clutching green glass bottles and singing along with a young man in a cowboy hat strumming a banjo. The Watcher does not understand what lemon-lime soda has to do with hayrides and singing. He would not have made a very good advertiser. The ideas seem to float too freely. There is no tangible way to apply them. Perhaps it is the realm of the artist, not the craftsman.

He glances outside cell 138 at the corridor of B block. The guards are elsewhere on their rounds. Gingerly, he fishes underneath his thin mattress for the blade he has separated from his safety razor. He works the blade as close as he can to the magazine's binding and, with a single even stroke, slices the advertisement free and slips it under his mattress. In this way he flips through the magazine, removing every second or third advertisement with surgical precision. He leaves the articles alone so nobody else gets wise to the fact that pages are missing. Tomorrow, he will return the magazines to the library.

In the cell next to him, Allen West whistles "Row, Row, Row Your Boat." At this signal, the Watcher hides the razor blade. A moment later, the young guard, Fuller, strolls by his cell. He stops and looks in. The Watcher, reclining, keeps his eyes on the magazine.

"I don't care if it's just a gopher snake," Fuller says. "I see one, I'm turning tail."

The Watcher lowers the magazine to peer at the guard over the top of the page. "How's that?"

Fuller tries on a rueful smile. "I guess you didn't get to that one yet."

The Watcher examines the cover of the magazine. At the very top it says, *Our most misunderstood snake, page 96.*

"I read it last night," Fuller explains.

"I suppose now I don't have to," the Watcher says.

"Sorry," Fuller says.

"Go jump in a lake."

The young guard scowls and moves on. West changes his tune to "London Bridge Is Falling Down"—the all clear. The Watcher gets up and takes the separated magazine pages over to the sink. The simple, repetitive melody lodges in his head and digs up an old memory. One of his foster siblings, a girl whose name he cannot recall, warbling off-key.

He shoves the memory down as he turns on the tap. In a moment the pages are a soggy mess. Using a spoon, he mashes them into pulp. He keeps working the spoon into what used to be magazine pages until there is only a clumpy substance the color of pencil shavings. He adds a bit of soap and a touch of glue. Then he listens. Nothing from West next door. Still clear.

Quickly and quietly, he takes the slurry in his hands and plops it down on the small steel table next to his bed. If someone were to glance inside his cell, it would look like the Watcher was kneading dough. After a while, this homemade plaster begins to congeal and harden enough to mold with his hands into the rough shape of a human head. He is absorbed in his work. He is no artist, it is true, but as he uses the spoon to sculpt the fore-head and eye sockets, he thinks again of what might have been. How oddly pleasant to lose himself in the soothing action of molding and kneading and shaping. A nose and the curve of a mouth begin to appear.

It is then that he realizes "Row, Row, Row Your Boat" is once again trilling out of West's cell. He does not know how long his neighbor has been whistling. He should not have given Fuller a sour kiss-off earlier. The young guard is very green and gener-ally meek, but it had been foolish to do something that might stick in the man's craw. He might get a notion to hassle the Watcher, maybe even toss his cell.

In defiance of every rule he has followed over the past few weeks—most importantly, never expose the escape hatch until the cover of darkness—the Watcher scoops up the soft plaster head and slides the accordion case aside with his foot. He stoops down and places the head into the darkness beyond the wall. The hole has been widened so that a man of the Watcher's stat-ure can crawl through. He slides the accordion case back into place and begins washing his hands. With his back to the cell door, he can sense Fuller step up and pause, staring daggers.

The Watcher hunches his shoulders, leaning over the sink, blocking the guard's view. He rubs the magazine pulp away from his hands, but it is too thick to vanish entirely down the drain. He is aware that time is ticking by while Fuller stares at him. He forces himself to step away and dry his hands on the scratchy towel hanging from the edge of the cell's single metal shelf. There is a ring of plaster caked around the drain. Nothing he can do about that now. He cannot poke at it right in front of the guard.

In the cell next door, West goes silent. No need for a signal when Fuller is right there.

The Watcher turns to face the guard. He puts on a disarming half smile. "Seems to me, looking just like a rattler's the best thing that ever happened to the gopher snake."

Fuller is not picking up what he is putting down. The glare fixed to his face is too overcooked. The Watcher pegs the young guard as an eager kid who wants to make his bones. Maybe show off in front of his superiors, play the tough guy. Inwardly, he curses. To have made it this far, chiseling out an escape hatch with a nail file welded to a spoon! Plotting with West and the Anglins, managing those other personalities, keeping the whole thing under wraps. And now it is about to be blown sky high—all because of some stupid snake article in *Popular Science*.

Jimmy the Hat is going to kill him. Literally.

"What's that on your hand?" Fuller says. He gives his baton a twirl. The motion is not entirely smooth and the baton clanks against the bars.

The Watcher pretends to glance down idly. His heart begins

to pound. A glob of homemade plaster is stuck to the skin between his thumb and forefinger.

"Mashed potatoes," he says. The dining hall did not serve mashed potatoes tonight. He hopes Fuller is not the kind of person who will check on something like this. He brings the hand to his mouth and eats the plaster. It tastes like soggy cardboard. Then he sits down on his cot and picks up a dime novel.

Fuller does not move. The Watcher opens the book to the first chapter. The words might as well be gibberish.

"What were you doing at your sink just now, inmate?" Fuller's voice takes on a note of authority the Watcher has never heard from the young guard before.

"Washing my hands," the Watcher says.

"Well, you did a bang-up job."

"Look, Fuller, I'm—"

"Open cell one-thirty-eight!" Fuller shouts to the guard stationed at the levers at the end of the cellblock. From there, guards can open and close a single cell, groups of cells, or every cell on the row. The Watcher closes the book. This is it: Fuller is coming in. All the guard has to do is take one look at the plaster clogging the sink drain and he will know something is fishy. Then it is only a matter of time before he moves the accordion case and discovers the escape hatch.

"Cancel that order!" a loud voice booms down the row. The cell door remains shut. A moment later, a big lunk of a guard is in Fuller's face.

Hiram Carter. The Watcher composes himself. He betrays no sign of relief.

"Mr. Fuller," Carter says, "until your probationary term is complete, you will not enter an inmate's cell without backup. Is that clear?"

"Yes, sir!"

To the Watcher's mild amusement, Fuller does not protest in the slightest. His back straightens and he stands at attention like he is an army recruit. Some of the other inmates on B block snicker. The Watcher holds his tongue.

"Now, what's going on here?" The Watcher has to hand it to Carter. He is awfully smooth for a big galoot.

Fuller hesitates. "This inmate had, um, dirty hands, and . . ."

Carter's eyes narrow. "What's the infraction?"

"Um . . ."

"Mr. Fuller, I think I can handle things from here."

"Yes, sir." Fuller moves on down the row. Carter waits until his footsteps recede. The cellblock hums with the activity of the hours before lights-out. Someone plucks a halting melody on an out-of-tune guitar. Carter moves closer to the cell. The Watcher stands up to meet him near the bars. He eyes the big guard's face and wonders about the long-ago punch that broke his nose. Did Carter see it coming? Did he feel it, or was he knocked senseless?

The Watcher lowers his voice. "I need paint," he says. "Flesh-colored. Four tubes."

"Tidy that worktable, inmate!" Carter says loudly, for the benefit of any eavesdroppers. Then he turns and walks away without another word.

The Watcher reclines on his cot and bunches up the thin pillow behind his head. The mattresses in Alcatraz are five inches thick, the pillows about five centimeters. He picks up the dime novel. *The Wayward Heiress: A Jake Hall Mystery.*

He has read a few other potboilers featuring Jake Hall. He has also learned from the magazines in the prison library that they made a television show called *Hall of Justice* starring the fictional private investigator. He allows himself a rare moment of sweet anticipation. After he breaks out, he will find himself a nice place with a featherbed—a mattress two feet thick—and a goose-down pillow. He will crawl in and watch *Hall of Justice* and sip a Coca-Cola through one of those bendy straws.

He smiles to himself. The escape has moved beyond a plot for its own sake, a diversion to get him through the days and nights on the Rock. The world beyond the island is invading his thoughts. He is no different from West and the Anglin brothers now, dreaming of life on the outside. He has warned them against too much talk of freedom, but still they pine after juicy steaks and big cigars and coffee that does not taste stale. Now here he is, dreaming of a comfortable night with one of the hundred television shows he has never seen.

The escape plan has moved to a new phase, beyond the realm of fantasy. All those feverish nights digging through the wall, the days spent refining methods, have delivered him here, to this moment. He realizes, finally, that he does not simply want to prove to himself that he can do this. He desires everything that comes along with it, everything his fellow inmates have wanted all along.

Speeding down some coastal highway with the wind in his hair.

Lying on his back in the desert while shooting stars blink in and out across the night sky.

Dancing with a pretty girl.

A warm feeling courses through him. The words on the page swim together. His eyelids, suddenly heavy, begin to droop. His mind drifts to the hole in the wall behind the accordion case and what is hidden there, in the darkness of the shaft.

A final piece of the puzzle.

A face of pulp and glue and soap, soon to become his.

CHAPTER

hip sets two chocolate milks down on the coffee table next to the newspaper. A politician smiles up from the front page, a man named Richard Nixon, who has just won his party's nomination to run for governor of California.

Chip sits down on the couch. The wooden birds of his mother's flock rise, forever frozen, pinned to their wood-paneled sky. The small clock with its mirrored face tells him it's three minutes to nine. His father is still on shift up at the prison. Outside, the wind howls through the trees.

Chip keeps an eye on the clock while his thoughts roam the city across the bay. He imagines dark tendrils slithering through the streets, unseen by passersby, knitting together in an unbreakable web. At the center of this web is the back room of the Andromeda Café, where Jimmy the Hat sits and schemes.

A chill descends. He shivers and it passes.

Two minutes to nine. He takes a sip of his chocolate milk, gets up, turns on the television just as the doorbell rings. He glances one last time at the second chocolate milk and goes to the front hall. The bell rings again.

When he opens the door, Maddie rushes inside, clamping a pink pillbox hat to her head.

"Wind's trying to blow me straight into the bay," she says. Chip shuts the door behind her.

"You came," he says.

She hands him her hat and tosses her jacket over the banister. "You sound surprised."

He won't admit it out loud, but until the doorbell rang, he was only half-convinced she would show up.

"Nice hat," he says.

"My mom calls it her First Lady hat. She said I could wear it. Guard it with your life."

He ushers Maddie into the living room and sets the hat carefully on the end table next to a lamp. She tucks her hair beneath her headband and sits down on the couch.

"That's for you," Chip says, nodding at the chocolate milk. To his astonishment, she drains it in one gulp, then swipes the back of her hand across her mouth.

"Nestlé Quik?"

"Yeah."

"That's the bee's knees. We don't have it at my house."

"It's starting!" He scrambles to the couch and sits down next to her. On TV, the opening credits fade up from a black screen: a cartoon city, skyscrapers with scowls and mean mugs, menacing a tiny figure fleeing through streets of deep shadow. The figure grows in size as he runs toward the viewers. He scrambles around a corner, trenchcoat flapping, as a hand darts out of an alley, missing him by an inch. The giant buildings gnash their teeth. Newspapers spin with wild abandon, then freeze to shout their lurid headlines. The man bursts through the pages. Words disintegrate into letters, then scatter and re-form into a stairway. The cartoon man sprints up them two at a time, then down a dizzying corridor. He bursts through a door and slams it shut behind him. Suddenly, the cartoon landscape switches to the real world. The nameplate on the frosted glass says JAKE HALL—PRIVATE INVESTIGATOR.

Massive words take over the screen as music swells: HALL OF JUSTICE.

Maddie looks sideways at Chip. "You invited me over to watch TV?"

"I invited you over because we need a new plan."

"Jimmy the Hat expects us to burn down the warden's house! We need more than a plan; we need—"

"Shhh! Wait for the commercial break."

Maddie grumbles to herself but sits back with her arms folded. On TV, Jake Hall is asleep on the sofa in his office, fedora hiding his face. His suit is rumpled, tie half-undone. He snores peacefully.

The office door opens slowly and silently. The music is all

tense, churning violins. A woman tiptoes inside. She is tall and slender, wearing a hat with a floppy brim.

Chip sucks in air through his teeth when he realizes who it is. "Candy Kincaid," he says.

"Who?" Maddie asks.

On TV, Candy Kincaid goes to the cluttered desk and slides open a drawer. It squeaks. She freezes, glancing at the sleeping detective. His mouth moves, whispering too softly to hear. Then his snoring returns. Candy opens the drawer the rest of the way and begins shuffling papers.

"They used to be partners," Chip explains. "All the way back in the first episode. But then she left the detective business for a life of crime."

"Is that why he always works alone now?" Maddie says.

"It's complicated," Chip says. "Shhh!"

"You talked first," she mutters.

Candy shuts the drawer and moves on to another one.

"The Webber file's in the cabinet," Jake Hall says. Candy looks startled, but only for a moment. She puts her hands on her hips and waits for him to sit up. When he does, a small pistol appears in his hand. He pushes his hat back on his head and flashes a grin. "Feels like a dream, you popping up like this."

"Good dream or bad dream?"

"Both."

"Lose the heater, Jake. I'm not here for trouble."

"You broke in."

"Your door was open."

He glances at the door. "I gotta get that lock fixed."

"You always were a step behind. I'm not here for the Webber file." She hesitates. Her voice softens. "I got a problem, Jake."

Chip looks over at Maddie. She's pretending to be annoyed, but he can tell she's getting into the show. They both watch as Candy tells Jake about the bank president she was blackmailing who was found drowned in his bathtub. Candy insists she's innocent, but she knows the cops will zero in on her soon.

Suddenly, there's a commotion on the stairs. Jake helps Candy flee out the fire escape. A moment later, a trio of cops barge in. Then it cuts to a commercial.

"Okay," Chip says, turning to Maddie. He has rehearsed what he wants to say, but now he finds the words getting caught in his throat. He takes a sip of chocolate milk and tells himself to just go for it. The worst that can happen is she walks out. "When we were in the city I came up with a plan, and you were pretty much right. It wasn't great. So, this time, I wanted to ask you to help me. Or just come up with one yourself, if you want."

"So," she says, looking him right in the eyes, "are you officially not working alone anymore?"

"It's not really about *working*." She waits for him to continue. *Here goes*, he thinks. "It's more about . . ." he stumbles. "I just thought, it might be something friends do. Put their heads together, instead of one just *deciding* how things are gonna go."

"Chip, are you asking me to be your friend?"

His heart is pounding. "Yes."

She laughs. He wants to shrink down to the size of a coin and roll into the couch cushions. She must be reading the look on his face, because she gets serious. "No, Chip, I didn't mean to laugh.

I'm sorry. You don't have to ask, you know. I mean: yes. We're already friends."

"Oh," he says. "We are?"

"After that day in the city? Of course we are!"

"Right," he says, flooded with relief. "Of course."

"Plus, without your dumb plan, we wouldn't know about the Alcatraz escape, and what our dads are really up to."

"We also wouldn't have to burn down the warden's house," Chip points out. "Plus, now that we know about the escape, if we don't report it, we're in big trouble, too."

"I thought about that."

"So what do we do?"

"What if we—"

"Shhh!"

The commercial break ends and *Hall of Justice* fades in. For the next ten minutes, Chip and Maddie watch Jake lie to the cops and press Candy for more information so he can help her clear her name before another commercial break cuts the tension.

"Wow!" Chip says. "So, what's going on is, the bank chief was laundering money for Jake's dad, a master criminal whose face we never see. It's Jake's life's mission to find him. See, back when he was a teenager—"

"I got an idea," Maddie says, standing up and pacing to the end table. She picks up the First Lady hat, then sets it down again. Outside, wind bends the trees, and branches scrape the windows. She pushes her headband back on her head. "Jake Hall's gonna team up with this Candy Kincaid, right? Even though he's a detective and she's a criminal?"

"Yeah," Chip says. "It happens a lot in his"—he shakes his head—"*our* line of work. It's not like the good guys and the bad guys have signs. Everybody's kind of in the middle."

She paces over to the wooden flock and pokes a beak. "I think we might have to do the same thing."

Chip's puzzled. He tries to figure out what angle she's working. "You mean, team up with a criminal?"

"The closest we've got to one, anyway."

"You don't mean—"

"Albert McCain."

CHAPTER

INSIDE

The cellblock is never quiet, even after lights-out. Guards' footsteps echo down the steel-and-cement corridors. Men cry out in their sleep—tough customers during the day reduced to scared little boys when the nightmares come.

There are other sounds, too—the groaning of the old penitentiary building as it stands up to another night of swirling winds. The *scritch-scratch* of rats nobody ever sees. The haunted whispers from the old military prison, Civil War ghosts refusing to take their rest.

The Watcher is confident that his movements will join this uneasy chorus. Even if some of the guards hear him, they will not know exactly what they are hearing. They certainly will not imagine the inhabitant of cell 138 is moving through the prison's hidden places like a blood cell through an artery.

The young guard, Fuller, moves past the cell, performing his count. The Watcher waits another minute, then creeps out of bed, moves the accordion case aside, and retrieves the plaster head. Thanks to the flesh-colored paint delivered to him by Hiram Carter, the decoy head could pass for his twin—at least in the dark. He tucks the "neck" into the sheets and lays the head against the pillow, mussing the hair collected from the prison barbershop by Clarence Anglin. He bunches up the sheets so they appear to be covering a sleeping body. Then he gets down on his knees and crawls through the hole beneath his sink. Once he is in the dark space behind the wall, he pulls a string tied to the accordion case, moving it back over the hole. He takes a moment to breathe and slow his racing heart.

There is no going back now.

He stands up carefully and waits for his eyes to adjust. Eventually, the utility corridor takes shape around him. It is still very dark in this narrow space behind the cells, but the Watcher can make out dull, paint-flecked pipes and old crusted valves. Wearing socks to dampen the noise and stepping lightly to avoid leaving prints in the grime, he moves along the corridor. The smell here is different from the prison, just on the other side of the wall to his left, where men live and sometimes die.

Once, as a boy, he waited out a terrible storm in a mausoleum. It smelled like this: dank and musty and lifeless. The smell of a place that sees long years between human visits.

The Watcher inhales with something like excitement. The odor means safe passage. He is not likely to encounter anyone else in here. As he moves along, he tries to forget that his cell is now occupied by a decoy head of homemade plaster and paint. All it will take is a guard on routine patrol lingering with his flashlight, noticing the head's odd pallor, taking a moment to study the curves and lines of a face that is just slightly *off*.

The Watcher casts the worry aside. There is nothing he can do about it now except stay the course. He enters a maze of plumbing, a nest of pipes lit from above by the weak glow of the house lights on the uppermost tier. Above him is the grate of a flat catwalk.

He grabs hold of one of the thicker pipes and hoists himself up, squeezing his lean frame between the catwalk and the wall of the utility corridor. He has the brief and unwelcome sensation that he is creating vibrations in the pipe that will echo out through the cellblock. It is almost amusing how easy it is to let his disciplined mind slip into fantasy, now that he and the Anglins and West have come so far in this plot. His very presence in this corridor, where discovery by a guard would lead to the whole scheme unraveling, jolts him like a cup of strong coffee.

He scrambles over the edge of the catwalk. There is a metallic popping noise, then a creak, like the settling of some great ship. It occurs to him that perhaps the rats the inmates hear but never see are actually *men* creeping between the walls. Other prisoners with similar plans, more sneaky blood cells in the veins of the old penitentiary. He shakes his head, dismisses this notion as crazy, and gets softly to his feet.

It does not take the Watcher long to find his way up to a second catwalk, then a third. Now he moves through sickly fluorescent half-light, like some forgotten wing of a hospital. To his left, above his head, the concrete wall gives way to a strip of wire mesh. This is where the upper-tier lights shine in. He finds another pipe to climb and sticks his head above the concrete rim, just high enough to see over the top. From here he can look out across the ceiling of cellblock B, all the way to the west gun gallery.

He takes a moment to appreciate the thrill of this like a normal person on the outside might appreciate a mountaintop vista. A new way of seeing the world that makes the narrow confines of routine and drudgery seem insignificant. It almost makes him laugh out loud like a madman. He wishes West and the Anglin brothers were here. Soon enough they will be, he reminds himself.

The single guard stationed at the gun gallery has his back turned. The Watcher's eyes follow the man as he patrols toward cellblock D. Then the Watcher lowers himself down. Just ahead is a mesh cage. Curious. He opens a screen door and steps inside. He glances down at the grate beneath his feet and waits for a dizzying sensation to pass. He is looking straight down into a ventilation shaft. If the grate were to give way, he would plummet from the height of the uppermost tier to the bottom row of the cellblock. There he would lie, dead or badly broken at the bottom of the narrow shaft, until someone figured out where he was.

The Watcher is not afraid of heights, but it is an unpleasant notion. He quits looking down and looks up instead.

This is a much more interesting view. The top of the shaft extends around a corner. It is one of those hidden interior spaces that does not make much sense. A sort of secondary air shaft that runs along the ceiling. The Watcher reaches up. At five feet seven inches, he can place his hand inside the strange, empty space, but he cannot see very far into it. He will need West or one of the Anglins to help him up there. He knows one thing: The horizontal shaft is directly underneath the roof of the building. Somewhere, there will be a weak point. An access hatch or some kind of ventilation cover.

This has been a fruitful trip. The layout of this hidden place is in their favor.

He forces himself to take one last look around, then climbs back down through the labyrinth of pipes to the lowest tier. He finds his way back to the hole behind his cell and pauses with his hand on the accordion case. There is a chance he will push it aside to find half a dozen guards waiting for him. But what else can he do? Every step now is a step that must be taken.

He nudges the case so that it slides quietly along the floor. He peers through the hole. The cell is dark. Next door, West is snoring. The Watcher lets out a breath he had not realized he had been holding. He wriggles through and stashes the decoy head behind the wall before putting the case back. Then he slips into bed and closes his eyes. His mind is churning with excitement. Eventually, he drifts into a jittery half sleep. What he could not see beyond the opening to the final air shaft looms large in his dreams. Again and again he feels himself climb out onto the roof where the cold wind lashes his skin. From there it will be a mad scramble down to the edge of the water and freedom . . .

The next morning he sits bleary-eyed at the table with West and the Anglin brothers. He cuts his sausage links methodically while West, already done, scrapes his plate.

The others are waiting for him to report on his trip behind the walls. The Watcher plays it cool. He does not want to get the three men too riled up. There is still much work to be done if they are to succeed. The last thing he needs is a man like West jumping the gun.

"The good news is," the Watcher says, "with all that mess of plumbing, it's no trouble to get up to the top tier. What's even better is that there's a little cage up there, out of sight of the gun gallery, at the top of a ventilation shaft. Means we can store our gear in there."

The men look relieved. This has been a major source of tension: how to keep their equipment out of sight.

"I'll start bringing up raincoats," John Anglin says.

"I got enough liquid plastic for ten rafts," Clarence says.

"All right," the Watcher says. "And here's the rub: Once we start moving on that, we gotta go *soon*."

"I agree," West says. "The longer we keep all this stuff around, the more risks we're taking."

The Watcher nods at Clarence, the tallest man among them. "I need you up there with me to give me a boost into the air shaft so I can scope it out."

Something flashes in Clarence's eyes. *Fear*, the Watcher thinks. The hesitation of a man who had not expected to be called into action so soon. The others look at him.

West smirks. "I'll go if you want."

"I don't care who goes with me," the Watcher says, "but we have to find a way up to the roof and we have to do it tonight. Otherwise we'll have to rethink this whole plan."

Clarence shoots daggers at West. "I'll go. You get your beauty rest."

"All right," the Watcher says. He looks at Clarence. "Tonight."

Clarence nods. "Tonight it is."

CHAPTER

23

hip and Maddie wait till the end of the day to approach
Albert McCain. They figure he'll be in a better mood when
school's over.

When the boat returns to Alcatraz, they follow him off.
The afternoon clouds part to throw scattered patches of
sun across the pier. Now that their plan is taking shape, the
landscape Chip has been surrounded by his entire life feels
strange. Building 64 and the social hall and the warden's
house—structures as familiar as the rocks themselves—all
seem like cardboard models.

They wait until Albert is climbing the steps to Building 64 to
make their move.

"Hey, Albert," Chip says.

The seventh grader wheels around. They are on a small, square landing, halfway up the staircase. "You tailing me, Carter?"

Chip moves a toothpick from one side of his mouth to the other. After surviving Jimmy the Hat, the older boy seems much less fearsome. Though, Chip supposes, getting socked in the face is still getting socked in the face, no matter whose fist it is.

"We need to jaw with you a bit," Chip says.

Albert folds his arms and shifts his glare from Chip to Maddie. "If this is about those stupid raincoats, I'm gonna lose my mind."

"Forget the raincoats," Maddie says.

"You know what, I don't think I can." Albert shakes his head sadly. "That hurt me, Thompson. I expect it from your brother, but not from you."

"You leave Benny alone!" Maddie practically shouts. Chip is stunned by her outburst. They're exactly one minute into carrying out the first stage of their plan, and already it's going off the rails.

Albert laughs. Chip sizes up the older boy's enormous hands, assuming that no matter how sore Albert gets at Maddie, he will be the one taking the punch. "*Me?* Leave *him* alone?"

He shakes his head at Maddie's blank face. "Lemme guess, you think I'm the big bad wolf, taking the poor kid's lunch money. You and everybody else on this rotten island."

"You *are* taking his money!" she says. "It's a fact!"

Chip shoots her a look. "Maybe we should say what we came to say, Maddie."

"Maybe you should leave me alone." Albert turns his back and starts up the stairs.

"Wait!" Maddie races up, brushes past him, and wheels around to stare him down. Her anger flares, then she pushes it aside. "We need to ask you something."

"So ask! I got a bowl of Sugar Smacks waiting for me."

Chip bounds up next to Maddie and cuts to the chase. "How would you like to start a fire?"

His eyes narrow. "I'm listening."

"It'll be soon," Chip says, "but we won't know exactly when until day of."

"We need you to burn something on the parade ground that makes it look like the warden's house is on fire," Maddie says.

Albert starts to laugh, then looks puzzled. "You are both a couple of crazy bedbugs."

"Imagine looking at the island from the city," Chip says. "Say, Russian Hill. Or even the pier. If somebody was standing there, and you had to convince them the warden's house was on fire, could you do it?"

"Without actually setting the house on fire," Maddie specifies.

Albert folds his arms across his chest. *At least he isn't storming off,* Chip thinks. This might actually work.

"So, lemme get this straight," Albert says. "You want me to start a fire on the island that fools somebody over in the city into thinking the warden's house is on fire."

"But you're not actually burning anything down," Maddie says.

"Or hurting anybody," Chip adds.

Albert turns and looks up. Chip follows his eyes, tracing the lighthouse and the mansion that rests on the island's highest plateau. Albert scratches his buzzed head, lost in thought. His gaze lowers to the parade ground, just off to their left. Then he turns and looks out across the water. Finally, he faces Chip and Maddie, regarding them with suspicion.

"Yeah," he says. "Of course I can do that. But you want this done so bad, why don't *you* do it, *detectives*?"

Chip glances at Maddie. "We have to be somewhere else," he says.

"Uh-huh. And if I get pinched, it's reform school for me while you two are sitting pretty. So how you gonna make it worth my while?"

"You can have my lunch money, too," Maddie offers.

Albert smacks his own forehead. "I don't *want* your lunch money, Thompson. I don't want your brother's, either, but he owes me big-time for swiping my grandpa's World War One medal."

"Benny wouldn't do that," Maddie says.

"Oh yeah? Maybe you don't know him as well as you think you do. I took it to the social hall last summer to show Roger, and Roger's an idiot so he lets Benny see it, and the next thing I know, it's gone."

"How do you know Roger didn't swipe it?" Chip asks.

"Because Roger's my friend, and Benny's a weirdo."

"If I track down the medal, will you help us out with the fire?"

Albert snickers. "Sure, gumshoe. I'll do this for you, but then you're on the hook for the medal."

"Deal," Chip says.

"Anything else, or we done here?"

"We're done," Maddie says.

"Go eat your Smacks," Chip says.

They wait until Albert vanishes around the bend to trudge up the rest of the way. At the top of the stairs, Maddie stops. Building 64 is behind her while Chip's cottage is down the path in the opposite direction.

"I guess we're all in now," she says.

Chip tries to reassure her. "It's a good plan." He gives a weird little wave that he immediately regrets. "Guess I'll see you tomorrow."

Maddie hesitates. "You think it's true?"

"What?"

"Benny and the medal. You think he'd really do that?"

Chip flashes to the jittery kid who came to his house the day this whole thing started, trying to warn him off the case. "I don't know. But after this is over, we'll find out. Together."

Maddie tries to smile. "Our second case. We're gonna need a real office."

She turns and heads for the apartment building. Chip watches her go for a moment, then makes his way along the gravel path toward the little cluster of cottages. The sun warms his face, and he moves slowly, enjoying the short, pleasant interlude. His thoughts unwind into a single thread. *This is going to work*, he tells himself.

As soon as he walks into the empty house, his mood takes a dive. The *San Francisco Chronicle* is on the table by the front door. The big headline on the front page proclaims GANGLAND SLAYING. Beneath the headline is a photo of a body being pulled from the water. The caption says "Reputed Lanza family soldier Sebastian 'Zipper' Kelly found dead by paddleboat tourists."

Chip lets his backpack fall to the floor. He can't tear his eyes away from the photo.

This is what Jimmy the Hat does to his own men when they cross him. If this plan fails, what will he do to Chip and Maddie?

CHAPTER

INSIDE

larence Anglin steps into the mesh cage atop the utility corridor with slow, careful reverence. To the Watcher, Clarence looks like a man setting foot in a church for the first time. The Watcher reminds himself that for people who have spent years locked inside Alcatraz's numbing routine, new surroundings are almost holy.

"I'll be," Clarence whispers as the Watcher joins him inside the small workshop space. "It's like they put it here just for us. It'll be perfect for makin' the raft."

"Long as nobody decides to poke their heads in before we shove off," the Watcher says, "we're golden."

In the light filtering in through the eaves, the two men move like wraiths in a fairy tale. They drag the shadows around with them. The Watcher lets Clarence bask in the moment. He knows what the man is thinking because he had the same thoughts when he first arrived. *Halfway to freedom. Maybe three quarters.* He gives Clarence thirty more seconds, then nudges him to get moving. Not one but *two* decoy heads back in their cells doubles the chances the guards will catch on.

"Come on, boost me up there."

The Watcher points up to where the mesh cage gives way to the air shaft that runs along the ceiling and curves out of sight. Clarence kneels down and bends his back so that the Watcher can put both feet on his shoulders. He braces his palms against the side of the cage and walks his hands up slowly as Clarence straightens up. He pokes his head into the air shaft. There is a new odor here. Perhaps it is his imagination, but the Watcher swears he catches a whiff of the sea.

As Clarence reaches his full height, the Watcher slips all the way into the air shaft and slithers on his belly. He is not claustrophobic, but it is an uncomfortable sensation, knowing that he is crawling through a narrow tunnel three full tiers above the floor of the cellblock. He rounds the bend. Darkness crowds in. His eyes adjust. He turns over and shimmies along on his back. There! A soft glint just above him. Steel bars. Two of them, covering a round ventilator hatch the size of a manhole cover. His heart begins to race. It is large enough for them to fit through. This is their passage up to the roof.

He studies the edges of the hatch. Big metal rivets hold it in place, like the ones you would find bolted into a ship's hull. He reaches up and tests the integrity of the hatch. It does not budge.

The bars can be spread and popped off with a ratchet tool from the workshop. He can smuggle one up here, easy enough. But the rivets are going to be a problem.

He makes his way back to the edge of the air shaft and dangles his feet out into the cage. Clarence's hands grab his legs and situate them on his shoulders. The Watcher descends.

The Anglin brother is practically vibrating with eagerness. "So? What's the verdict?"

The Watcher tells him about the ventilation hatch. "The bars are no sweat. It's the rivets that're giving me the gringles."

"Nah," Clarence says. "A drill's all we need. Take 'em right off."

"Gluing together a pile of raincoats is one thing, but I don't wanna risk running a motor up here." He pauses. "Lemme think about it."

The next afternoon, the Watcher flips through a stack of old *Popular Science* magazines until he finds what he is looking for. He waits till the big bruiser of a guard, Carter, is making his rounds. He beckons him over with a quick hand gesture.

"Inmate," Carter says. "What'd I tell you about that worktable?"

"Keep walkin', Carter."

Carter leans in toward the bars.

"Carborundum," the Watcher says quietly. The guard blinks. The word hangs between them. It is as if the Watcher has requested a blowtorch. Or a sniper rifle. Carborundum is the most closely guarded item in the machine shop: an abrasive cord with diamond-hard grains that will cut through almost anything. It is used only for closely supervised repairs, dispensed and retrieved by guards who measure and record each usage. "One foot's all I need," the Watcher says.

The guard does not change his expression. His gaze lingers. Then he is gone.

CHAPTER

Time after Zipper's murder passes in a blur. Every day, Albert gives Chip and Maddie a questioning look on the boat. Every day, they shake their heads.

Not tonight.

Now it's Monday, June 11—the first day of the last week of school before summer break. Chip wonders how Jimmy the Hat will get them a message once school's out. He imagines a carrier pigeon with a little scroll attached to its scrawny leg, landing on Chip's windowsill. Wings shiny with olive oil, a tiny fedora perched on its head, a cigar stuck in its beak. He smiles to himself, lets the fantasy unfurl.

"Chip."

Maddie's voice is distant, coming at him from some deep

cavern. He imagines the carrier pigeon pecking a little hole in the sill, bored and agitated while Chip reads the note. The sea-birds of Alcatraz Island swooping in for a closer look at this tough character from the big city.

"Chip!"

Maddie's elbow gives his arm a sharp nudge. He shakes off the imaginary pigeon. Reality hits hard. A dismal sensation creeps in. He can feel it everywhere, even in his teeth and behind his eyelids. There's a reason he's been spending more time chasing dreamy thoughts to whimsical places. His inner life is an escape from what's hanging over them like the blade of a guillotine, waiting to fall. Instantly, he wishes he were back with the imaginary pigeon.

"I could really use a root beer float," he mutters.

Chip and Maddie are lagging behind the clump of Alcatraz kids hustling up the Embarcadero, double time, toward the pier. Their chatter, spiked with peals of laughter and wild shouts, sweeps back over him with the sea breeze. A familiar energy swirls around the last week of school, the heart-bursting joy of pure freedom and possibility. While everyone else lets loose, jitters are all he feels.

Next to him, Maddie whacks the trunk of a palm tree as they pass it by, a thin echo of his dad hitting the heavy bag.

"I asked my brother about Albert's grandfather's medal," she says as a streetcar glides alongside them. Chip glimpses strangers' faces, profiles in silhouette.

"All those people, going different places," he says. "And they've all got problems. Some of them even bigger than ours, maybe. You ever think about that?"

"Are you listening to me?"

"Yeah," he says, turning away from the streetcar as it picks up steam and disappears around the bend in the wide road. "Sorry. What did Benny say?"

"He says he didn't take the medal. He says Albert's just a no-good bully."

"You believe him?"

She hesitates. A ragtag crew of college-age kids runs across the road in tight black jeans, sunglasses, and beret hats like French people. One of them carries a guitar slung across his back. *Beatniks*, Chip thinks, watching them straggle out toward the piers.

"I would have believed him before all this, no sweat," she says. "But now I don't know what to believe. It's like everybody I thought I knew turns out to be somebody different. That *Body Snatchers* thing again."

"Well, the body snatchers didn't get us," Chip says.

"I'm not so sure. A couple weeks ago, I was just like everybody else. Now look what I'm doing."

"I don't think you were ever normal," Chip says. Immediately, he regrets the way it came out. "You weren't like everybody else. I just mean . . ." he says, struggling to find words that won't make it worse.

"That I'm some kinda weirdo?" she completes the thought and starts to laugh.

Chip, his face hot, laughs along with her. "Some kinda *beatnik*."

"Hey, maybe I will be someday."

"I think you have to like poetry a whole lot."

"Maybe I do."

He gives her a sidelong glance. "Do you?"

"Maybe," she says. He leaves it at that.

Just ahead, a man on a bench turns the page of his newspaper. A pair of old ladies on roller skates glide effortlessly past. A boy sitting on the curb hits bongo drums with wild abandon while his mangy dog howls. Two blocks up, Chip can see the older kids from Building 64 toss a baseball between them in high arcing lobs. *Life*, he thinks. No matter what happens to Alcatraz, the city will go on and on and—

"*Pssst.*"

The man on the bench folds down a corner of the newspaper as they pass him. A familiar mug glares out at them. Cold eyes, mouth in a hard thin line. Startled, Chip's hands go up instinctively.

Freddie.

"*Tonight,*" Freddie says. Then he hides his face behind the newspaper. His knuckles are swollen and bruised. Chip thinks of Zipper's body being pulled from the water. He doesn't move until Maddie drags him away.

INSIDE

Everything is in place.

The Watcher brushes his teeth at his steel sink and tries to fool himself into thinking it is like any other Monday night in Alcatraz. He has been here for hundreds of them, after all. He believes that if he operates the same as always, it will help blunt the adrenaline surge. He does not think of the word *escape*. He does not imagine the cold wind off the water, or the cries of the gulls, or the crash of the waves on the shoreline. He does not think of his grand plan to sip a Coca-Cola while he watches *Hall of Justice* in a nice hotel room.

Lights-out comes at 9:30, just like every night. The cells go dark and the only illumination filters down from the upper-tier lamps. He and the boys will have some time before the cellblock quiets down. Thirty or so minutes to reach the roof, when any noises they might make in the utility corridor will be hidden among the clamor of men winding up their conversations and plucking out a few last melodies on banjos or guitars. The Watcher sits on his bed and takes it all in. He is just about to reach a calm state of deep focus when his neighbor summons him with a harsh whisper.

He goes to the edge of the cell closest to West's. "What is it?"

West sounds nervous. "You know how word came down the guards were doing random cell searches over the weekend?"

"What of it?"

West takes a breath. "Well, my grate cover I dug out kept slipping down when I put it back in place, so I packed in a little fresh cement behind it to hold it."

The Watcher grits his teeth. He knows where this is going. "Great."

"It was just supposed to be enough to hold it together, easy enough to pop back out tonight. Except . . ."

"It's not so easy."

"I must have used too much."

The Watcher's calm darts away like a minnow. Months of work, and now this. At the same time, there's a rustling down underneath his sink. The accordion case begins to move. The Watcher glances up and down the cellblock. All clear. He rushes over to slide the case out of the way.

John Anglin pokes his head into the cell. "Last raft's leaving for Angel Island. You coming?"

"West's trapped," the Watcher says.

Anglin curses. "It's now or never. Jimmy the Hat'll have us skinned alive if we don't go tonight."

Frank returns to the edge of the cell. "We got the two rafts," he reminds his neighbor. Clarence had brought up so many raincoats from the basement, they had managed to patch together a spare raft with all the extra material. "We'll leave one up there in the cage for you, if you manage to dig yourself out tonight. But we gotta go, West. You know how it is."

"No!" West's voice rises into hysteria. "You can't leave me here!"

"Cut the gas, West!" the Watcher growls in a low voice. "You're gonna get us all popped." He finds that he does not care if West makes it out or not. They will all be splitting up once they reach the mainland anyway.

West has enough presence of mind to shut his mouth. The Watcher knows he will never see the man again. West is now part of his past and he is looking to the future. Quickly, he tucks in his decoy head, bunches up the sheets, and joins the Anglin brothers in the corridor behind the cells. He pulls the accordion case back against the wall to hide the hole.

The Anglins move like men being chased. They shimmy up the pipe with frantic energy, their feet scrabbling for purchase. The Watcher curses silently. First West, now the Anglins. He will have to be first out of the ventilation shaft to take the lead to the shoreline. The brothers are liable to get them all shot.

In the mesh cage atop the corridor, the Watcher looks out across the ceiling to the west gun gallery. It is dark, the post empty for the night. Silently, the men gather up the makeshift raft and a pair of homemade wooden paddles.

The Anglins give each other a look the Watcher cannot read. As men who grew up together and have rarely been apart, the two brothers have their own way of communicating. A language of gestures and expressions known only to them. He wonders if they will stick together or split up.

Without a word, Clarence kneels down and the Watcher steadies himself on the taller man's shoulders. He works his way up the mesh and crawls into the ventilation shaft. When he reaches the hatch, he snaps the six bolts off one by one. It is not difficult: His careful sawing with the carborundum supplied by Hiram Carter has left each one hanging by a thread. He wonders idly what will happen to the guards who aided their escape, Carter and Thompson. He does not dwell on it. He does not really care. They are part of his past now. Behind him, Clarence hoists his brother up and then John reaches down to pull Clarence into the shaft. It is awkwardly done and the Watcher cringes as the narrow tunnel resounds with the noise of flailing limbs.

"I'm going up first," he whispers to the men. "Follow my every move. I crawl, you crawl. I run, you run. And for God's sake, keep quiet out there."

He removes the hatch cover, exposing an even narrower vertical shaft. He wedges his shoulders inside it and begins to stand up, ever so slowly. After a moment his head brushes against the thin grate lying over the hole in the roof. He keeps rising and finds that he is not only dislodging the grate but wearing it, along with its rain hood, like a hat. He tamps down his excitement. *Still a long way to go.* Then several things happen at once.

The lighthouse flashes, nearly blinding him.

A gust of wind blows across the island, snatching his strange headpiece and slamming it down to the roof, where it lands with a clatter.

Roosting seagulls, spooked by the noise, take to the skies as one great squawking mass.

The Watcher ducks back down into the shaft and waits for the sirens and the searchlights he knows will be coming any second as the tower guards zero in on his position.

CHAPTER

Chip stands on his porch and gazes out across the dark expanse of the parade ground. *Nothing yet.* He can only hope that Albert McCain is out there somewhere, preparing his decoy fire. Chip and Maddie had given him the nod on the passenger launch earlier this afternoon. Albert had kept his cool, but Chip could read the gleam in his eye.

He tries not to think about the end of the last Jake Hall episode. Candy Kincaid helps Jake track down his father while Jake helps her clear her name for the murder of the bank president. Then, in the final scene, just when you think they might actually partner up again for good, she leaves him high and dry. And he realizes she took the Webber case file with her—the one she claimed she never wanted in the first place.

Betrayal. It's a chance you take in this business.

Chip shoulders his backpack and sets off toward Building 64. He doesn't look up, not even a quick glance. He doesn't want to see the warden's house, or the pale white shape of the prison sitting heavy in the darkness. At the place where the gravel path turns into the stairs down to the island's lowest level, Maddie huddles against the railing. When he gets closer, he realizes she's traded her Mary Janes for a pair of boots.

"Hey." He keeps his voice just above a whisper.

"Hay is for horses," Maddie says. "You got it?"

"I got it." He nods at the satchel slung across her body. "You?"

"Every last drop."

They descend through the night, down into the brick and stone of the old dungeon alley.

"This is where I first tailed your dad," Chip says. "That day with the raincoats. Seems like a million years ago now."

Instead of turning south to the beach just down the cliffs from the cottages, where he'd followed Mr. Thompson, Chip and Maddie head north. They creep past the pier where the passenger launch is tied to the dock. Then they leave the path entirely, working their way along the scrub that frizzes out from the rocks, just above the waterline. They pass beneath the lowest windows of the social hall. Inside, bowling balls hit the lanes with dull thuds. Music he can't make out leaks from a half-open window.

"My dad's in there tonight," Chip says. "Weird, for a Monday."

"Mine's at work," Maddie says.

Chip thinks for a moment. "I guess it makes sense for at least one of them to be off. Might be suspicious if they were both on the night of the escape."

It's a strange feeling, knowing his father is only a few dozen feet away. He's glad when they put the social hall behind them. The rock face is steeper here, and they cling to the scrub as they work their way around the powerhouse to the north side of the island. Flashes from the lighthouse barely reach this desolate shoreline. Off to the left, the Golden Gate Bridge twinkles in the fog like Christmas lights hanging from the eaves of the night sky.

They scramble down from the scrub onto a flat strip of smaller rocks. The bay pounds the surf.

"They're just up here," Chip says, pointing to a trio of large cubes in the shadow of the powerhouse.

"I know," Maddie says.

Every kid on Alcatraz knows where the lumber is stored. Massive pallets of two-by-fours and other useful pieces of wood, kept dry under tarps away from the water's edge. Nobody ever seems to notice if you snag a few pieces for a Soap Box Derby car or a fort.

Chip unslings his pack and removes sticks of kindling, strips of blond wood no bigger than Jake Hall's club. He begins to pile them around the base of a lumber stack. Maddie watches with her hands on her hips.

"I know this is my plan," she says, "but now that we're here, maybe we should just forget it."

"Don't worry," Chip says. "It's a good plan."

"That's what you said last time, too."

"Last time I was lying."

"That's aces."

He finishes arranging the kindling and turns to look at Maddie. "Listen, you got it all pegged. You can't see this side of the island from the city. Even if the Hat's standing on a pier with binoculars, Albert's fire will hide any smoke from this one. Meanwhile, with two fires going, the warden'll have to call all the guards out to see what's going on down by the water. The escape will go bad, but Jimmy the Hat won't know it's our fault. So, we're square with him, plus we keep the bad guys from getting off the island. It's duck soup all the way around."

He watches Maddie straighten her posture as she gathers her courage. He is grateful that of all the kids on this island, the best one chose him for a friend. Warmth spreads from his belly to the tips of his fingers.

"For our dads," she says, pulling the plastic container of lighter fluid from her satchel. She sprays the kindling, moving back and forth around the lumber pile. The pungent stench mingles with the salty air of the bay. Chip's head swims.

Maddie squeezes the container till it runs dry.

Chip pulls a box of long fireplace matches from his backpack. He touches one to the strike pad and pauses. "For our dads."

Maddie nods.

Chip lights the match.

CHAPTER

OUTSIDE

The Watcher's name is Frank Morris.

Now the Watcher is part of his past, like Allen West and the guards and cellblock B and the lousy coffee in the dining hall.

There is no more watching. Only doing.

He has been holding his breath in the ventilation shaft, sweating despite the cool air rushing down the hole. Morris resolves, at that moment, that he is never going back to his cell. He will let the tower guards shoot him if it comes to that. At least it will be some kind of freedom. But the sirens never come. No alarm is raised. Perhaps the racket up here had been muffled by enough cement that it had barely sounded inside the cellblock. Whatever the reason, it is once again time to move. There is no turning back.

"Now," he whispers, and pulls himself up to the roof. Clarence passes up the raft, folded into a long rubbery roll. How strange that it used to be a pile of raincoats. A moment later, all three of them are huddled next to a skylight frame that juts up like a pyramid. The radiant burst from the lighthouse flashes every five seconds. Morris turns to the Anglins and mimes a crawling motion. The brothers nod in unison. With Morris leading the way, the three men set off for the edge of the roof. They are in view of the guard in the north gun tower, but thanks to the steep line of sight, the closer they get to the tower, the less visible they will be.

Will there be a warning shot? A command to *STOP*? Or will the guard simply fire on them? He tries not to think about a bullet ripping through his spine. He crawls over the edge and drops down onto the roof of the mess hall. Immediately, he lowers himself flat and slithers over to the kitchen vent pipe jutting up from the side of the building. He does not consider what he is about to do. Thinking about it will only make it worse. He hitches the raft to his belt, scrambles over the side, and shimmies fifty feet down the pipe. He does not look down. When he hits the ground, he curls into the deep shadows at the base of the mess hall.

Tomorrow, the other inmates will trudge to the canteens for their coffee. Same as yesterday and the day before that. But Morris will be long gone.

A moment later the Anglins join him. He points across a flat expanse to the cyclone fence. The north tower looms. Morris tells himself the guard would have to lean out and look almost straight down to see them now. Still, he does not take chances. He leads the Anglins in a slow army crawl to the fence. Then he climbs the links and navigates the loosely coiled wire at the top. On the other side, the three men move past the water tower and down a sharply angled cliff for twenty or so feet. They work their way around to a small cove, hidden from the gun towers and anyone else peering down from the prison. The breakers lapping the shoreline are *loud*. Morris realizes how muffled and hollow everything sounds inside the cellblock. Out here, the vastness of the ocean has a frequency. A primal rush in his ears he has not heard for a very long time.

"Carter says there's lumber out here for the taking," Morris tells the other men. "A couple boards'll shore up the raft."

"There!" John Anglin points to some hulking shadows, cube shaped and covered in tarps. He starts up the beach, but Morris grabs his arm.

"What's that?"

The three men peer into the darkness. There is something up there, Morris is sure of it.

"Raccoons?" Clarence offers.

"You ever heard of a raccoon on the Rock?"

Clarence falls silent. Morris picks out two distinct forms.

A match flares.

CHAPTER

As Chip bends to the fuel-soaked kindling, Maddie cries out in alarm. Some reflex makes him blow out the match flame. A split second later, his arms are seized from behind and he's wrenched back from the lumber. The shock of the sudden attack is dizzying. He kicks out into the air. It's no use: His captor's grip is iron. The world spins. He catches a passing glimpse of Maddie being whisked away, down toward the waterline. It's impossible to tell how many people have jumped them. The night is a haze of fog and distant light.

A hoarse whisper sounds in his ear. "They're just kids!"

He's facing the water now. His captor allows his feet to come down to earth. He meets Maddie's eyes. A lanky man as tall as his father pins her arms behind her back. Chip assumes a similar figure is holding him fast. That leaves one more person: a shorter, compact man who steps between them.

"Listen to me," this man says calmly, looking from Maddie to Chip. "You didn't see us. You weren't here. You were home in bed, where you belong."

The man holding Chip jerks his arms. Pain shoots down his back. "They're gonna blab the second we let 'em go."

Chip wishes he could say something brave, like *You'll never make it!* or *The sharks will eat you!* That's what Jake Hall would do: look death in the eye without blinking. He finds that in this moment, he doesn't much care if these three inmates actually make it off the island, or if they get caught, or if the bay claims their lives. All he knows is that the case that began with a bunch of stolen raincoats ends here.

"Well, we can't take 'em with us," the man in the middle says.

"We won't say a word," Maddie assures him. Chip knows she is doing the right thing: telling the men what they want to hear. It's the only way out.

"Not if you're face down in the bay, you won't," says the man holding her. Chip wishes he could reach for Maddie's hand. He stomps down hard on his captor's foot. The man grunts and tightens his hold.

"So we just take one of 'em, then," Chip's captor says. "A hostage might come in handy."

The man in the middle ignores his two comrades and looks from Maddie to Chip. "You just have to keep your mouths shut for a few hours. In the morning they'll find us gone anyway, and by then it won't matter. Can you do that?"

Chip wishes he knew why these men were sent to Alcatraz. Are they killers? Jake Hall would do everything he could to prevent killers from walking free—even if it meant sacrificing his own life.

He decides to tell this man to go jump in a lake. But before he can get the words out, his captor whips around. Someone's approaching—fast. Heavy footprints clomp along the rocks at top speed. A burly figure in a white undershirt glowing with reflected moonlight rushes up the shoreline and comes fully out of the darkness.

"Dad?"

Before Chip can get the word out, his father leaps toward him at incredible speed. His fist rockets through empty air. There's a sickening *THUNK*, along with a *crack* that can only be a nose breaking. The grip on Chip's arms loosens entirely and falls away. His captor crumples to the rocks, out cold.

Chip turns, astonished, to see his father loom over Maddie's captor, who is backing away toward the water. His father's massive fists are like boulders. The third man, the one Chip thinks of as the negotiator, faces down Chip's father with his arms out, as if to say *Calm down, please*.

"Easy there, Carter," he says.

The sound of his last name coming from this man's mouth makes Chip feel queasy. Everything is happening too fast. He fights the urge to stand perfectly still and let numbness take over. He moves alongside his father to face Maddie's captor. She's his friend, and he will not let her down.

"Let her go, Anglin," his father says to the man holding

Maddie. "Now." Anglin looks toward the negotiator, who nods.

He gives Maddie a shove. She staggers up the rocks. Chip rushes over to put his arm around her and keep her from falling. At the same time, he keeps a close eye on his father.

Hiram Carter could be a hero, right now. The man who stopped the great Alcatraz prison break. Chip's former captor is still out cold. As far as he can tell, the other two men are unarmed.

"All right, Carter," the negotiator says. "You know how this has to go."

Chip waits for his father to slug the man. For a moment, nothing happens. Then his father unclenches his fists.

"Yeah," his father growls. "I do. So get going."

"No, Dad," Chip says. "We can stop 'em right now!"

Chip's father turns to face him. The look on his face breaks Chip's heart. He shakes his head. "It's gotta be this way, Chipper."

The negotiator laughs, cold and mirthless. "Sorry, kid. No hard feelings."

The man goes to his fallen comrade and drags him down to the waterline. Meanwhile, Maddie's former captor bends to what looks like a puddle of rubber at his feet. He extracts a long plastic tube and begins to blow into it, just like Mr. Thompson had done that afternoon on the opposite side of the island. Slowly, the makeshift raft inflates.

Hiram Carter gathers up Chip and Maddie. He turns them around and begins walking them gently back the way they came. Chip tries to look back at the men escaping Alcatraz Island, but his father blocks his view. Half a minute later, they round the bend and put the cove behind them.

"It's going to be all right," his father says.

Chip doesn't think that's true, but he keeps his mouth shut. The low clouds that have been wisping through the sky begin to drape across the island. His father ushers them through the scrubgrass on the slanted rocks below the powerhouse.

The foghorn blows.

CHAPTER

30

OUTSIDE

Morris perches in the front of the raft, clutching the paddle with two hands. John Anglin is dead weight, curled up at his back. Clarence shoves the raft into the water, sloshes forward up to his knees, then clambers inside. The raft tilts crazily. Morris still cannot believe what just happened with those kids and Carter coming out of nowhere. There will be time to turn it all over in his mind later, when they are far away from Alcatraz.

For now, there is only the bay.

Keeping the distant lights of the Golden Gate Bridge to his left, Morris paddles wildly. He aims the raft straight at the dark mound of Angel Island, a mile and a half north of Alcatraz. The plan is to rest and recover in the deserted forest that covers half the island, then make their way across a narrow strait to the mainland. After that, he will split from the Anglins, steal a car and some clothes in Tiburon, and hightail it up through Northern California. Or maybe head east into Nevada. It does not matter right now.

There is only the bay. And the bay is angry. Back when he had looked out at the sea from barred prison windows, even the stormiest days had seemed more placid than this. Now that he is out here in the midst of the great roiling emptiness, waves that he would not even have noticed from up on the island batter the tiny raft like—

Well, like a million fists. Like Carter himself is pummeling them from the depths.

Morris paddles furiously. The raft pitches and rolls with the swells. Spray stings his eyes. Clarence shouts something from behind him. He cannot tell what the man is saying. All he can do is paddle.

What seems like hours later, Angel Island is still a dark mound on the horizon. How is it not getting any closer? He passes the paddle back to Clarence without a word and collapses in exhaustion. He is sure they made two paddles back in their mesh cage workshop, yet somehow they escaped with only one. A day earlier, Morris would have bristled at this lapse in concentration, but all he can do now is pull salty air into his lungs and gaze up into the madly careening sky.

They will make it. They have to make it.

Clarence, cursing and sputtering, fades away somewhere behind him. Endless waves slosh over the sides of their little craft. Raincoats held together with liquid plastic! That is all that stands between Morris and the depths. He is soaking wet. Water rushes in his ears. He imagines it as the sound of Coca-Cola fizzing in a glass. He licks his lips and instead of salt tastes sweet, sugary bubbles.

There is a whole world beyond this awful place. He wants to see it. He has never wanted anything more in his whole life. He makes a silent promise to be a better man. Behind him, Clarence is yelling something about the paddle. Morris thinks he might be saying the paddle is lost.

We'll paddle with our hands, Morris tries to say. But there is so much water in his mouth, all he can do is cough. *We can make it.*

The stars whirl above him. Then the stars and the sea become one.

We have to make it.

CHAPTER

Chip and his father deliver Maddie safely to Building 64. On their way home, crossing the parade ground, they pass a bonfire in progress. Six or seven older kids, whooping it up around flames shooting high into the sky. Chip can't see their faces, only silhouettes by the firelight. But he's certain there's a stocky seventh grader among them.

With the events on the beach crowding out every other thought, he'd forgotten all about Albert's mission. It had been a good idea for Albert to enlist some other kids. Even if they get in trouble, it seems less suspicious than a single unattended fire on the same night of a prison break.

He wonders what the bonfire looks like from the

mainland—if the angles are correct to make it seem like the warden's house is ablaze.

Of course, even if Albert set it up perfectly, the trick will last only until morning, when Jimmy the Hat will realize the mansion still stands, unscarred by flame. Chip has always known this, deep down, though he and Maddie never once brought it up. Their plans are not perfect. Probably, they are not even good. But no matter what happens, he will always know they tried. They followed clues like real detectives and did their best with the information they uncovered. And they did it together.

At home, by some unspoken agreement, Chip and his father both go straight to the living room. Chip takes an armchair, his father the sofa. Light from a single lamp carves deep shadows across the furniture. They do not even pretend to sleep. His father sips coffee. Chip eats a Baby Ruth.

His father speaks first. "Six fifty. That's when the morning count will go off. By seven o'clock, they'll know Morris and the Anglin brothers aren't in their cells. But they won't know if they got off the island. They'll call all of us in to search. I'll have to go."

Chip hears the words. He understands the meaning. But it's as if his thoughts are stuck on a loop. He sees his father, again and again, charging up the rocky shore in slow motion. He sees his father's fist pop Anglin's nose. He sees him scare the daylights out of the man holding Maddie.

Chip had been too young during his father's boxing career. He can't remember ever seeing him punch anything but the heavy bag in the room upstairs. But he knows his father would have beaten all three men to a pulp in order to save him. He could see it in his father's eyes. The rage. And the pain.

In return, Chip offers his father the only thing he has to give: the truth. Between bites of the chocolate bar, Chip tells his father the whole story, beginning with the day Maddie hired him to investigate a pair of "stolen" raincoats. He watches his father's reactions, sunk deep into the sofa, as he talks of eavesdropping on the poker game, tailing Mr. Thompson to the Silver Spoon, confronting Jimmy the Hat.

Following the threads.

When he describes Maddie's plan to fool the mob boss with one fire and foil the escape plan with another, Chip's father finally cuts in.

"Chipper, you could have come to me anytime. What you saw, and what you did . . ." He looks at the fist that had flattened Anglin and then sticks his hand between the couch cushions. "You're my son, and I love you so much."

Something flares deep within Chip's gut. A hint of anger? He's not sure. It doesn't seem fair to his father, but he tries to find the words.

"I couldn't talk to you," Chip says. "It felt so different, once I found out you were part of the escape plan. It's like Maddie said about her dad: *Body Snatchers*. I just couldn't believe it, I guess."

His father sighs. "I never thought it would get this far." He sets his coffee down on a coaster. "Well. I don't know what I thought."

"Why did you do it?"

"Jimmy the Hat's not a guy you say no to."

"I mean why did you play cards with gangsters in the first place?"

His father thinks for a moment. "Because, ever since your mother . . ."

Chip waits for his father to say it. *Died.* He wills the word out into the air. *Died. Died!* But he doesn't. Chip wonders if he ever will.

"Ever since then," his father continues, "I started realizing how *cold* this place is. I don't just mean the weather. I mean the whole island." He shudders. "The prison. All these sad men, pretending to be the toughest customers while a bunch of guys like me pretend to be even tougher." He shakes his head. "It's no place for you to grow up. I can see it in your eyes, Chipper. How you wish you were somewhere else. You're a special kind of kid, a real good egg, and this isn't the place for you. But it's like this: For a real fresh start, for us to go somewhere you deserve to be—I didn't want to wait too long, save up the slow way. I needed money."

Chip puts the rest of the candy bar down. Suddenly, he's lost his appetite. This whole thing had been for *him*?

His father seems to read his face. "I don't have too many skills," he says. "I got out of the service, and I fought till I couldn't fight anymore, and then the Department of Corrections came calling. I could have applied to transfer to another prison. Somewhere far away. But I dunno. It seemed like that would be more of the same. For both of us." His father shifts around on the couch. He looks down at his knees. "And maybe I don't like who I am too much anymore." He clears his throat and meets Chip's eyes with a wry smile. "Maybe you'll let me come live with you when you're a famous detective someday."

Chip tries to smile back. Tears blur his vision. "A big penthouse apartment in the city."

"Sure." His father laughs. "Why not?" He sips his coffee.

Chip settles back into the armchair. He wonders what's going to happen next, but he doesn't ask his father about it. The anger that flared inside him a moment ago is gone, replaced by something that burns like the bonfire across the parade ground. Something that has always been there, even when it's cooled to embers. But right now it's roaring back.

"I love you, too, Dad. I'm glad you were there today. On the beach."

His father stands up. "I was heading back from the social hall when I saw the two of you skulking around the staircase." He grabs a plaid quilt from the sofa and comes over to the armchair. "Couldn't resist seeing what a couple of detectives were up to."

His father drapes the blanket over him and pats his shoulder. "Get some rest," he says, and clicks off the lamp.

Chip curls up in the chair and closes his eyes. Somewhere in the darkened living room, his mother's flock watches over him from the wall.

He thinks of her now. He thinks of his father. He thinks of those three men in their tiny raft of raincoats, fighting the wind and the waves. He thinks of Maddie, just up the path in Building 64, and wonders if she's managed to fall asleep.

Time passes. He listens to his father pour another cup of coffee. He counts eight heavy footsteps to the living room, where they stop. He imagines his father leaning against the side of the archway, sipping coffee, watching over his son.

Before he drifts off, he imagines a frosted glass door high up in an office building with a nameplate that says CARTER THOMPSON DETECTIVE AGENCY.

EPILOGUE

The San Francisco Giants are in a heated pennant race with their biggest rivals, the Los Angeles Dodgers, and on this July evening, Candlestick Park is sold out.

Crack!

Dodgers second baseman Jim Gilliam pops it up. From his seat behind center field, Chip watches his favorite player, Willie Mays, wave off the other outfielders. The crowd begins to cheer as the ball comes down. Chip leans forward. He can't believe he's going to see this happen in real life, not just on TV.

Instead of raising the glove above his head to make the catch,

Mays lays it out, palm up, in front of his chest. Like magic, the ball drops down into it.

Every single Giants fan loses their mind.

"The basket catch!" Chip shouts above the din. "I can't believe it!"

In the seat to his left, Maddie stuffs a handful of buttered popcorn into her mouth and hands him the bag. She grins, kernels stuck in her front teeth.

Chip gives her a toothpick.

His father, on his right, gives him a nudge. "You want some more Cracker Jacks?"

"I'm okay," Chip says.

His father frowns. "I think I'll get you some more."

Chip smiles. "Dad, if you want Cracker Jacks, just admit it."

"They're for you!" he protests, and stands up. "I'll be right back. Sit tight. Don't get caught up in some new case while I'm gone."

Chip watches his father file awkwardly down the row.

"Like we can help it," Maddie says. She snaps the toothpick in half.

"Just doing our job," Chip says. Mays's catch was the third out, and fans are up and about for the seventh inning stretch. The stadium loudspeakers blare "Take Me Out to the Ball Game." Wind whips in off the bay. A little kid's orange cap sails out of the stands and down the third base line.

"Speaking of doing our job." Maddie shifts in her seat, jams a hand in her pocket, and wriggles it free. She presents a closed fist to Chip, then opens it. In her palm is a red-white-and-blue ribbon. Attached to the ribbon is a star-shaped bronze medal, detailed with a pair of crossed swords and a crown.

Chip blinks, taking it in. The ribbon is old and worn, the bronze lightly tarnished. He looks at Maddie. "Albert's grand-father's medal!"

She grins. "Our second case, open-and-shut."

"Where did you find it? Did Benny have it after all?"

"Nope." Her eyes gleam with mischief. "And you're not gonna believe who did. I went to—" Suddenly, Maddie falls silent. She looks past Chip to the seat next to him. Chip senses a presence there. By the look on Maddie's face, he guesses it's not his father. He turns.

It's Freddie, Jimmy the Hat's bagman.

Instantly, his heart pounds. He grips the sides of his seat as if he's about to be ripped away from the stadium.

Chip swivels his head up and down the row. Surely, his father will be coming back any second. But there is only a sea of fans crowding the aisles, carrying hot dogs and drinks.

"Relax," Freddie says. "I can't stay long. I got a message for you from Mr. Lanza. Your debt is paid. We're square. And nobody's the wiser about two guards who might've greased the wheels for the escape. Not the cops, not the feds, not J. Edgar himself. You want it to stay that way, you keep your mouth shut." He moves to get up from the seat.

"So those three guys got away?" Chip blurts out. There have been no reported sightings of the negotiator, whom Chip has learned is named Morris, or the two Anglin brothers. The pris-oners have not been recaptured, nor have their bodies washed up. But the escape must have been successful for Jimmy the Hat to wipe the slate clean.

Freddie smirks. "Maybe they did, maybe they didn't. All that matters is the powers that be are shutting down the Rock. For good."

Chip is astonished. Nobody else seems to know this yet. Not his father, or anybody else on Alcatraz Island.

"We got friends in high places," Freddie explains. "And Mr. Lanza is happy with the outcome."

Chip thinks of Jimmy the Hat's rage at the "festering barnacle" on the hull of his city.

"Neat trick with the fire, by the way," Freddie says. "Mr. Lanza thought it was funny." He levels his cold gaze at Chip. "Don't see me laughing, though."

"That's because you don't have a sense of humor," Maddie says.

Freddie glares. "Don't push it." He stands up.

"See you around, Freddie," Chip says.

"You better hope not."

With that, he's gone, moving down the row in the opposite direction. Chip lets out a breath and meets Maddie's eyes. He doesn't quite know what to say. He's relieved, yes, but it doesn't feel like an ending. More like the close of a chapter in the much longer story of the Carter Thompson Detective Agency.

The song ends, and the Dodgers take the field.

"We gotta have a lock," Maddie says. "For the office door."

"Can't have guys like Freddie just popping in," Chip says.

"A couple of potted plants, too," Maddie says.

"Yeah," Chip says. "And a coffee machine."

"I don't drink coffee."

"Me neither. But maybe the people who hire us will want some coffee."

"Does Jake Hall offer people coffee?"

Chip pauses. "Well, no. But our office will be nicer than his."

"Two desks," she says. "Two couches. Two filing cabinets."

Chip grabs a handful of popcorn. "So we never have to work alone."

AUTHOR'S NOTE

James A. Johnston served as Alcatraz's warden from 1934 to 1948. The boat that ferried residents back and forth to the mainland was named after him, both in real life and in this story. According to Warden Johnston, "the essence of Alcatraz is a maximum-security prison with minimum privileges."

In the early years, those privileges were indeed kept to a minimum. Inmates were allowed one visit per month, subject to the warden's approval. There were no newspapers or radios, and contact with the outside world was almost completely cut off. Prisoners were not even allowed to talk to each other while in their cells, and violating this "rule of silence" would result in harsh punishment.

It's no wonder people tried to escape.

The events in this book take place twenty-seven years after the prison's establishment. By this time, two other wardens had come and gone. Many of the rules had been relaxed. But the urge to break out of Alcatraz remained. There were fourteen escape attempts between 1934 and the final days of the prison in early 1963.

This book concerns the thirteenth attempt, the most complex and meticulously plotted. It's also by far the most famous, thanks to the enduring mystery: What happened to Frank Morris and the Anglin brothers?

The answer is that nobody really knows. The FBI launched an exhaustive investigation, which produced evidence to show that the three men survived, or that they drowned in the frigid bay, depending on who you ask and what *they* want to believe. Soldiers combed Angel Island and found nothing. None of the robberies in Northern California in the aftermath of the escape turned up any evidence that pointed to the men, even though they would urgently need clothes, food, and transportation upon reaching the mainland.

Unless, of course, they had outside help. I have taken some of the rumors associated with this theory—that guards were in on the plan, along with organized crime figures—and used them as the basis for this story.

Besides Morris, West, and the Anglin brothers, the only character taken from real life is Jimmy the Hat, who really did rule the San Francisco underworld, and whose family really did get rich from selling olive oil during World War II.

Chip, Maddie, their fathers, and all the other kids are fictional. Through them, I hoped to re-create the atmosphere of Alcatraz Island in the early 1960s as authentically as I could. That would not have been possible without the help of several books that explore Alcatraz from different points of view.

Alcatraz: A History of the Penitentiary Years by Michael Esslinger is both an incredible resource and a lively and engaging read. It's full of photographs and packed with fascinating stories from every stage of the prison's life. Esslinger writes that "the obsession to escape Alcatraz was consistent throughout the prison's history," and his book examines every one of the fourteen attempts in great detail.

Without J. Campbell Bruce's *Escape from Alcatraz*, I would not have been able to write the chapters from Morris's perspective. This book was an invaluable guide to the escape plan and inspired the raincoat "theft" that kicks off the mystery in my story. Bruce's account of the escape is full of wonderful details, from the carborundum string to the missing oar.

Two books helped me build the world of the island for the guards and their families. *Last Guard Out* by Jim Albright is a fascinating peek into the inner workings of the prison, and *Eyewitness on Alcatraz* by Jolene Babyak is an oral history as told by former residents of the island. These books brought the routines and habits of the Alcatraz kids into focus, from the boat rides to the social hall.

My story would not exist without the authors and works mentioned above. Any historical inaccuracies, geographical impossibilities, and tweaks to time and space should be blamed on me and me alone.

It's been an amazing journey through Chernobyl, Berlin, Stalingrad, and now Alcatraz with you. See you next time.